Mouse Woman
and the
Vanished Princesses

Mouse Woman
and the
Vanished Princesses

by

CHRISTIE HARRIS

DRAWINGS BY DOUGLAS TAIT

Atheneum · New York
1976

TO

the native peoples of the Northwest Coast
who gave us Mouse Woman

Library of Congress Cataloging in Publication Data

Harris, Christie.
Mouse Woman and the vanished princesses.

SUMMARY: Six legends of vanishing princesses and
the tiny character, sometimes mouse, sometimes woman,
who helps young people in many Northwest Coast Indian stories.
1. Indians of North America—Northwest coast of
North America—Legends. [1. Indians of North America—
Northwest coast of North America—Legends] I. Tait,
Douglas. II. Title.
E78.N78H34   398.2'0977   75-23147
ISBN 0-689-30502-8

Contents

How It All Started

IT WAS IN THE DAYS of very long ago, when things were different.

Then supernatural beings roamed the vast green wildernesses of the Northwest Coast. And people called them narnauks.

There was Raven, the Great One who could change himself into any shape he wanted, in order to trick people. And Raven's tricks were awesome.

At the other end of awesomeness, there was Mouse Woman, the Tiny One who watched the world with her big, busy, mouse eyes. She especially watched the tricksters. And she watched the young people they tricked into trouble. For of course there were people, as well as narnauks, living in the Northwest.

In fact, in those days, totem pole villages edged many lonely beaches. Standing with their backs to big snow-capped mountains, the villages were bright with the carved and painted emblems of the clans: Eagle, Bear, Raven, Frog, Wolf . . . And totem-crested canoes dared the wild rivers; they threaded the wild maze of islands; they ranged the wild coast from Alaska to California.

In some of the biggest houses and canoes, there were princesses. Daughters of high chiefs and chieftainesses, they carried the royal bloodlines; they would mother the future high chiefs and chieftainesses. So, on great occasions, the princesses put on gleaming fur robes, totem headdresses, and long woolen ear tassels glistening with squares of abalone mother-of-pearl.

Because they were precious to the great clans, the princesses were carefully guarded. Yet, somehow, they vanished. Again and again they vanished. Without a trace. And the alarmed villagers widened their eyes with dismay and whispered, "Narnauks?" to one another.

Mouse Woman, who was always watching, did not widen her eyes with dismay. She narrowed them. With purpose. And, as she considered what she might do, her ravelly little fingers often poked about for bits of wool. That was the mouse in her. For of course, she was Mouse as well as Woman. And though spirit beings needed to have things transformed into their essence, by burning, for full use, the mouse in Mouse Woman was so strong that she often snatched up woolen things as they were, and began to tear them into a lovely, loose, nesty pile of mountain sheep wool. It was the one improper delight of a very, very proper little being.

1

The Princess and the Feathers

FIRST, A WOLF CREST PRINCESS vanished from an upriver village. She vanished without a trace. And her clansmen from all the villages loped along the trails, alert for some sign of her. They searched the shorelines. They questioned travellers.

"Have you seen any sign of the Wolf princess?" they asked the travelling arrowmaker.

He was a strange old man who paddled from place to place with his marvellous arrows. And though he was as tall and as spare as any young paddler, his face was so wrinkled that he seemed to have lived forever. As if his skin had once been stretched over an enormous moonface, it now hung loosely over his shrunken features. It hung so loosely that, when he shook his head at their question, his wrinkles wagged like wattles.

"Haven't you seen anything?" the people insisted.

But the old man just shook his head again, wagging his hanging wrinkles.

Then, a year later, another princess vanished from another upriver village. She vanished without a trace. This time it was a Frog Crest princess. So Frog clansmen loped along the trails, alert for some sign of her. They searched the shorelines. They questioned travellers.

"Have you seen any sign of the Frog princess?" they asked the old arrowmaker. He might have. For he travelled widely; every hunter wanted an arrow winged with the golden feathers that only he knew where to find. He might even have glimpsed a narnauk, since he was a man who clearly had mystic powers. Wasn't there a mysterious power in his arrows? people whispered to one another. Perhaps he could put a spell on them. Or perhaps he used feathers from a Heaven Bird. Certainly there was magic in his golden-winged arrows. So he might have glimpsed a narnauk.

"Haven't you seen anything?" they insisted.

But the old man just shook his head, wagging his hanging wrinkles.

Then, a year later, yet another princess vanished from yet another upriver village. She vanished without a trace. This time it was a Raven Crest princess. So Raven clansmen loped along the trails, alert for some sign of her. They searched the shorelines. They questioned travellers.

"Haven't *you* seen anything?" they asked the old arrowmaker.

And once more he just shook his head, wagging his hanging wrinkles.

"Perhaps this is a cruel trick of Raven's," someone suggested.

Alarm gripped a coastal village near the mouth of the river. "For next it will be our turn," its people whispered, nodding toward their Eagle princess with anxious faces.

At least she never moved without her proper guard of friends-and-attendants, they noted with satisfaction. Two high-ranking Eagle girls always hovered near their princess, who was called Wy-en-eeks.

"It would be good to have Wy-en-eeks married," people muttered to one another. For then there would be a man in close attendance. Too, a married woman would be less attractive to some narnauk who wanted a human wife.

The next time the old arrowmaker arrived at their village, they questioned him sharply about the other princesses. "Haven't you seen anything at all?" they insisted.

But again he shook his head, wagging his hanging wrinkles.

As always, they wondered about the old man, who must be very wealthy. Great chiefs paid him so handsomely for his arrows that his house must be soft with furs and elegant with carved chests and painted screens, with beautifully carved bowls and hornspoons; it must glint with copper and abalone pearl. But no one had ever seen it. They only knew that it was hidden away on one of the many islands that fringed the coast near the river's mouth. The old man was as mysterious as his golden-winged arrows.

When he had sold his arrows, he paddled off without a word. And people turned their eyes back to the Eagle princess, a beautiful girl whose dark eyes flashed with spirit.

It was the time of wild roses. The air was fragrant with their sweetness. And women, back from their clam beaches, were readying their berry baskets.

Then a summer fog shrouded their world. And the Eagle princess was kept indoors.

"But why?" Wy-en-eeks fumed.

"You know why," her mother answered. "Fog makes it easy for some stranger to slip in and hide behind a rock or a tangle of driftwood."

"But the smoke is smarting my eyes," Wy-en-eeks protested.

A fire was burning in the center of the huge windowless house; and the shrouding of fog was keeping the smoke from rising up briskly through the smoke hole.

"I wish you were married," her mother said, as she had said daily.

"To Kuwask." Wy-en-eeks wrinkled her nose, just a little. But she knew she would marry Kuwask. It had all been arranged by their families. Indeed, she had only a few moons left of freedom. "Freedom!" she breathed, with a great sigh. And her spirit surged outdoors, toward excitement, toward new places and new people. For, with the blood of sea-hunting chiefs racing through her veins, the princess liked fast water and wild winds. She gloried in storms that clattered pebbles across the beach and set the waves smoking with blown spray. And she hated being housebound.

"Heeay!" a child cried, coming into the big house. "The sun is burning through."

"At last!" Wy-en-eeks said, beckoning her two attendants.

"You will be careful?" her mother cautioned.

"How can I not be careful with these two hovering round me like bears round a spawned salmon?"

"Like bees round a pink rose," one of her friends corrected fondly. And before handing it to her, she checked the princess's handbasket to see that it held her cosmetic stick and her little woman's-knife.

"Here is a light robe," the other friend said. For Wy-en-eeks was precious. Wisps of fog must not chill her.

The sun burned through quickly. And the girls strolled along the beach trail, pausing to sniff the roses. Then they sat on a driftlog, chatting about a handsome young man they had seen at a winter potlatch.

But Wy-en-eeks quickly switched the conversation to a handsome young man they had seen at spring trading. He was one of the lordly, flashing-eyed Haidas who had come over to the mainland from their big offshore islands to trade their superb canoes for the mainlanders' goatskins and hornspoons and oolaken fish grease. "I wish I could have gone home with him," she confessed.

Her girls looked at her with gentle disapproval. "Oh no, Wy-en-eeks!" Only a captured princess went home with the terrifying Haidas.

"No," she agreed. "I wish I could have *been* him." Paddling far out to sea. Leading great sea hunts or slave raiding parties. "Why must my life be so dull?"

"Your life will never be dull," her friends predicted.

"The fog will soon be rolling in again," one of them noted. "So let's go to the point and then turn back." She leaped the log, landed on a big loose stone, and turned her ankle. "No walk for me," she groaned.

At once, her friend began treating the sprained ankle.

"While you're doing that," Wy-en-eeks said, "I'll walk on to the point."

"But—"

"You'll see me every minute," she pointed out, with some impatience. And she walked off.

"Well . . . Keep in sight! You don't want some narnauk carrying you off, do you? Or even some Haida."

"Why not?" the princess called back; and she was only half joking. It might be very exciting to be carried off to some strange land by a glorious youth. Instead of just to an ordinary village by ordinary Kuwask. And for one wild moment, she wondered if the vanished princesses had helped themselves vanish.

Wy-en-eeks walked to the point and stood there, watching the sun touch the sea mist with opalescence. Then a flash caught her eye. Ahead of her, beyond the point, a wonderful man moved out into the full sunlight. He was tall. His pale robe caught the light with discs of abalone pearl and with a fringe of—Were they golden feathers? And his head shone. Dazzled by the brightness of the vision, she wondered if he had a cap of golden feathers behind his glistening ear ornaments.

With lips parted in wonder, Wy-en-eeks glided toward him. And caught in some spell, she kept moving toward him. As she neared him, however, her maidenly training touched her, so that she could not look fully at him. She only sensed that his skin, stretched smoothly over his lean face, was luminous, as though dusted with pearl shell.

Then he spoke. And his voice was vaguely hoarse. "Where are you going, Princess?"

"For a walk." Her voice was a dream voice.

"Shall I go with you?"

"If you like." She scarcely breathed it; for it all seemed unreal. As if she would awaken from her dream soon.

"Will you come to see my parents, Princess?" His words seemed to float around her. His parents? If he was taking her to see his parents, he was planning to marry her. Strange as it seemed, she was being carried off by a supernatural-being-in-human-form, as princesses had been carried off in the old tribal tales. And she could do nothing about it. She could not have said no. She could not have stopped moving along at his side. For her own will had left her. And it was strangely terrifying, yet delightful, to the princess who yearned for excitement.

She was led to a small but elegant canoe. And still in a dream state, she was engulfed in the warm softness of the white wolf fur robes lying in the canoe.

As he paddled silently off, toward the misting waters, a tingling mixture of awe and terror kept her eyes downcast. And swift, darting glances caught only the dazzle of pearl discs and golden feathers.

Then the fog began to close in around them. Wisps of mist moved like wraiths, silent and cold and eerie, shrouding the real world. Islands became vague, unreal shapes floating in a terrible silence.

"Princess," he murmured, "we can't reach my parents' house tonight. But I have a hut on a nearby island."

The hut was a small but beautifully carved

house. And when he led her in with his pitchwood torch, its richness caught her breath. It was soft with furs and elegant with carved chests and painted screens, with beautifully carved bowls and hornspoons; it glinted with copper and abalone pearl. Her glance roved about with pleasure as he kindled the readied firewood in the center of the house.

"Refresh yourself, Princess," he invited, opening a chest that was fragrant with sweet hemlock-sap cakes. "I must attend to the canoe."

He was so long in returning, the furs were so soft, the fire was so cosy, and the princess was so exhausted from all the excitement, that she fell asleep. Later, she sensed his return and murmured dreamily to him.

Then, suddenly, it was morning. And in the dimness of the light that came in through the smoke hole, she saw him lying asleep. The golden cap was gone. The hair was loosened. And—

Her gasp brought his head up. His hair slipped from its holder and—

His wrinkles slipped with it.

Wy-en-eeks shrank back. "You're . . ." She swallowed in horror.

"The Man-Who-Bound-Up-His-Wrinkles," he said, leering at her. He wiped pearl dust from his face and wagged his hanging wrinkles.

The princess was terrified. She had known the old arrowmaker had strange powers. But she had not known he was an evil sorcerer. And now he had her in his power. Her hand covered her mouth. And her tears fell.

"Why are you weeping?" His voice was hoarser now, and quick with suspicion.

"Oh . . uh . . ." She knew she must not anger him. "Because my family will be anxious about me . . . I can't stay here."

"No. You can't STAY here," he agreed. And his sudden laughter was the laughter of a madman. "I have other plans for you, my pretty princess."

"Plans?" She scarcely breathed it. And her hand slid silently toward her handbasket, where her little woman's-knife waited. But, seeing his sharp eyes watching her, she took out her cosmetic stick and pretended to care for her appearance.

Wy-en-eeks licked her dry lips. "You have plans?" she said, keeping the terror from her voice.

Instead of answering her, he opened a chest, took up a piece of dried salmon, and dipped it into an oil box. Then, after a long, horrible, chewing time, he said, "I will show you how I get my feathers."

"Your feathers?" she said, pretending bright interest. "Still . . . my father will be anxious." She hoped to remind him that *her* father was a very great chief, a man not to be angered lightly.

"I will show you how I get my feathers," he repeated, glaring at her.

"Oh. That will be . . . very interesting," Wy-en-eeks said. No doubt the other princesses had been shown how he got his feathers. And *they* had never come back. She kept her hand close to her handbasket as she readied herself to go out.

As she stepped into the small canoe—now stripped of its fine furs—her eyes were alert for some familiar landmark. But she saw nothing she recognized.

The fog had been washed away by a rainstorm. And now the sea and the sky were blue, and the snow-capped mountains. The clouds were as white as the surf and the flashing seagulls. And as they moved out, kelp heads bobbed, glittering dark brown in a sea that seemed suddenly deep and strange and terrifyingly lonely.

They rounded an island.

"That rock!" he said, so suddenly that she jumped. "I get my feathers on that rock."

It was almost an island. A grim, jagged gray mass thrust up from the sea floor. It seemed a strangely sinister place. For no seagulls wheeled and screamed above it. No seals poked up glistening heads around it. Instead, there was only uncanny stillness and silence. There was only one tree—the dead bones of one tree; and its skeleton arms seemed to wait for. . . . For what evil birds? Wy-en-eeks swallowed and clutched her handbasket.

Then she saw the small curve of a beach, a

beach that would disappear when the tide rose. He paddled straight to it. "Now you will see how I get my feathers," he said, motioning her out.

With the quick grace of a seagoing people, Wyen-eeks leaped onto the tiny beach. Then she turned, alert to cut the rope and grab the canoe while he was tying it to a boulder.

But, instead of leaping ashore too, the Man-Who-Had-Bound-Up-His-Wrinkles pushed off with the shriek of a madman.

"Now you will see how I get my feathers," he screeched at her. He held his scrawny arms up to the sky. And shouted.

"A LIVING FEAST! FOR YOUR GOLDEN FEATHERS!" he shouted.

Four times he shouted it at the sky.

"A LIVING FEAST! FOR YOUR GOLDEN FEATHERS!

"A LIVING FEAST! FOR YOUR GOLDEN FEATHERS!

"A LIVING FEAST! FOR YOUR GOLDEN FEATHERS!"

Then he paddled off, laughing with maniacal glee.

And her horrified eyes saw a small darkness, high in the air. As she watched, openmouthed, the darkness grew into a flock of birds.

SHE was the living feast. For THEIR golden feathers.

Wy-en-eeks glanced wildly about her. But where could she hide on a grim, jagged gray rock? A squeak caught her ear. Then a small flash of white caught her eye. A white mouse! It darted under a low ledge of outjutting rock at one side of the beach.

A cave?

She flung herself after the mouse. And there was a cave, a low, shallow cave. Frantic with haste, she wriggled into it, feet first. Then, grabbing a mat of golden brown seaweed to peep through, she pulled her head in just as the birds began to circle the dark rock.

They were horrible big birds with long glinting black beaks and scrawny yellow necks. But as the flock turned away from her, their backs glinted gold in the sun. And as she watched, peering through the seaweed, she saw a fall of feathers, like a golden snowfall.

For their golden feathers!

But there was no *living feast* waiting for them.

They rose as one and circled the rock four times, screaming in unearthly fury at the offending rock.

Wy-en-eeks shrank back. And her teeth were chattering. Her limbs were trembling. They would find her. Or, if they didn't find her, they would wait. And the tide would rise, flooding her shallow cave with the icy water that not even the strongest man could live in for long. The water was already trickling in. She felt its icy wetness on her body.

Silence.

Had they gone?

She dared to peer out again through the seaweed.

No. They were not gone. They were settled like the Fruit of Death on the skeleton tree.

She swallowed. And waited.

The tide was rising. Already its cold was numbing her.

Then, again, that SCREAM of fury. She covered her ears and her eyes as she heard them circle the rock again, four times.

Then—at long, long last!—the sound faded away, upward.

The birds were gone. And the girl, almost as terrified of the rising tide as of the gruesome birds, crawled out of the shallow cave. Faint with fright, she lay against the slanting rock, letting the sun warm her.

What if they should come back? Now! When there was no place to hide.

There was no sign of the birds. And no sign of the terrible old man and his canoe. But *he* would come back to gather his feathers and gloat over her bones. He would see her, and call down the terrible birds again. Wy-en-eeks glanced round in panic. Perhaps there was another hiding place? Now that her cave was flooding.

Scrambling wildly over the rocks, she came suddenly on a small pile of bones, with a handbasket

lying near them. A basket with a Wolf crest! Those were the bones of the vanished Wolf princess.

Trembling with terror, and searching wildly for a hiding place, Wy-en-eeks scrambled this way and that. She came on two more piles of bones, with two more handbaskets.

But she found no place to hide.

Though she shrank back from the golden feathers, she made herself gather up a few of them. And with a prayer that they would have power for her, she put them into her handbasket, close to her little woman's-knife. If she escaped, she would have proof of the evil deeds of the old arrowmaker.

The day stretched on and on and on, endlessly, while the tide crept up the rock.

Then the tide began to ebb. And her terror grew, waiting for the old man. He would come when the beach surfaced again. But what if he came after slack water? When her cave was flooding again! When there was no place to hide.

As she watched the seaweed laid bare on the rocks, hope sprang up. Perhaps she could gather a great pile of it. Enough to cover her. She began frantically pulling it free.

He did not come with the evening low tide. And the brief darkness of a northern summer night brought her respite. For he would not come in the dark to gather his golden feathers.

It was low tide and morning when she saw his canoe rounding the island. She could hear him singing. It was a mad, jubilant singing. It reached her ears as she wriggled part of her body back into the cave, and as she covered the rest of her body with the golden brown seaweed. Then she held still, her hand clutching her little woman's-knife.

No doubt he was catching the glint of golden feathers on the rock, for his song grew wilder. He paddled straight to the little beach, leaped out, and tied his canoe to a boulder. Still singing his mad song, he began scrambling up the rock.

Almost holding her breath, Wy-en-eeks waited.

He was well up the rock before she dared to jump up, slash the rope, push the canoe off with all her might, and leap in. She grasped the paddle and plied it with all her strength.

He heard the grate of the canoe. And with a shriek of rage, he came tearing down the rock.

But Wy-en-eeks was well offshore. She was out in the deep numbing water where not even the strongest man could live long.

"I came to get you," he yelled at her. "I came to take you home to your father. I haven't been able to sleep, worrying about you. So I came to get you."

"You came to get the feathers," she shouted back at him. And for a moment, she dared to stop paddling.

"And now," she screamed at him. "Now you shall give the feast you promised them for their golden feathers. Now you shall die as the princesses died. As you meant me to die."

Holding her arms up to the sky, she shouted as he had shouted.

"A LIVING FEAST! FOR YOUR GOLDEN FEATHERS!" she shouted. Four times she shouted as he had shouted.

"A LIVING FEAST! FOR YOUR GOLDEN FEATHERS!

"A LIVING FEAST! FOR YOUR GOLDEN FEATHERS!

"A LIVING FEAST! FOR YOUR GOLDEN FEATHERS!"

Wy-en-eeks shrank down into the canoe as she saw the small patch of darkness, high in the air. Then, with a gasp of fear, she plied her paddle, rushing away from the rock as the small darkness grew into a terrible flock of birds with long glinting black beaks and scrawny yellow necks. She heard the wild screams of the old man. And in near panic, she scanned the passing islands, looking for some familiar landmark.

At long last she saw a point of land she recognized. And she fled straight for home. Soon she saw the canoes that were out searching for her. But only when her small canoe had grated on the pebbles of her home beach did she drop her paddle and sink down in utter exhaustion.

Voices were crying out for joy. Arms were lifting her. Warm robes were engulfing her. "Wy-en-eeks! Wy-en-eeks!" her mother was sobbing in relief.

"Where is my father?" Wy-en-eeks asked her. "He is being comforted by his friends," her mother answered, pointing toward a house at the far end of the village.

But already the great chief was on his way to greet his daughter.

She took a golden feather out of her handbasket.

"A feather of the old arrowmaker," people gasped, crowding about to see it.

"This is what the princesses died for," Wy-en-eeks told her father. "What it was meant that I should die for."

"The feathers of the old arrowmaker," people murmured to one another. "HE took the princesses."

"Invite all their fathers," Wy-en-eeks said. "And I will tell them about their daughters."

Messengers leaped into their canoes and raced upriver to the grieving chiefs and their families. And when they were all gathered in her father's house, Wy-en-eeks told her story. And clan dirges wailed through the great cedar house.

Next day, all the people went with the Eagle princess to the terrible rock.

First, her family landed on the tiny beach to gather the golden feathers. And then, while the others went sadly onto the rock to gather up their vanished princesses' bones, her family went on to the house on the island to strip it of its riches. For, in those days, things were done in the proper way. Then the family returned to the village to prepare for the grieving people.

Once more in her father's house, Wy-en-eeks put on her robe of white wolf fur. She put on her Eagle headdress and her glistening abalone ear ornaments. In the ring of sea lion bristles that circled her headdress, she put eagle down, the symbol of peace and friendship. And she danced a graceful dance of welcome for the grieving guests, dipping her head to waft a snow of eagle down over the families.

Then her father, with great ceremony, divided the golden feathers and the old arrowmaker's riches among the chiefs who had lost their daughters. For, among proper people, those who had been deprived must be compensated, to keep all things equal.

Suddenly, to everyone's amazement, a white mouse appeared from nowhere. And in a scurrying, merry little dance, it circled the fire four times.

"The white mouse!" Wy-en-eeks called out. "The white mouse who helped me!"

But the white mouse was gone. And in its place stood a tiny old woman in a dark mouseskin robe. She gazed about at the people with big, busy, mouse eyes. And her nose twitched.

"Mouse Woman!" people cried out. Then they hushed themselves in awe. For Mouse Woman was a narnauk.

But already Mouse Woman had vanished.

Or had she vanished?

Wy-en-eeks felt a tug at her robe. And there stood the tiniest of narnauks.

"You were the one who helped me," the princess cried out in delight. "I should have known it." For wasn't Mouse Woman the one who always helped young people who had been tricked into trouble? "You helped me, Grandmother."

"Yes, my dear." The voice was a squeaky little sound in the hush of the great house.

Then Mouse Woman seemed to stand waiting. For what?

"Of course," Wy-en-eeks breathed, remembering her manners. For Mouse Woman was known to be a stickler for proper behavior.

"Of course," the princess breathed again. For those who had given service were to be given something in return. The obligation of a gift, including the gift of service, was sacred in the Northwest. It was the great law that kept all things equal.

She took an ornament from her dark hair—a golden feather tied with a cluster of prettily dyed woolen tassels. It was a proper gift since the wool held the spirit power of the mountain sheep it had come from; while the golden feather held who-knew-what power. And with graceful ceremony, she handed it to the little old woman.

There was a gasp from the people.

Wy-en-eeks glanced about in alarm.

Then she flushed with concern. For, of course, she should have tossed the gift into the fire to transform it into its essence for the use of a spirit being like Mouse Woman. She turned anxious eyes on the imperious little narnauk.

But Mouse Woman was busy. Her ravelly little fingers were tearing the prettily-dyed woolen tassels into a lovely, loose, nesty pile of mountain sheep's wool. And her soft sigh showed that this was strangely satisfying.

Then, while Wy-en-eeks's mouth was still open, the tiniest but most proper of all the narnauks vanished.

2

The Princess and the Bears

FOR MANY YEARS no princess had vanished.

But Mouse Woman was keeping a sharp watch with her big, busy, mouse eyes. She knew plans were afoot. And she meant to thwart the planner.

"It's not proper to trick a princess and carry her off from her family," she told the planner. And her voice was as tart as crabapple.

It was in the Place-of-Supernatural-Beings, high in the mountains. And the tiny old woman was standing on a big rock to be at eye level with the handsome young man she was scolding. (Though that put her almost at eye level with his woolen ear ornaments, which she was itching to get into her ravelly little fingers.) "Also," she went on, "it's not proper for the Prince-of-Bears to marry a mere human."

"Is it proper for mere humans to slaughter my

bears just to show off their skill as hunters?" Prince-of-Bears countered.

"Of course not," Mouse Woman squeaked. "But their cruelty has nothing to do with marriage."

"It has everything to do with marriage," the handsome young man assured the tiny old woman. "Their cruelty angers the bears. Anger brings on trouble. And what do humans do when trouble is brewing between two groups? I'll remind you, Grandmother. They arrange a marriage and turn enemies into relatives, who then *have* to care for each other."

"A proper thing to do between two groups of humans," Mouse Woman answered. And her nose twitched.

"Who would know me from a human?" he challenged her.

"Any sharp eye would catch that amble in your walk," she retorted. (Her fingers moved toward the enticing tassels, then pulled back.)

"But what girl has a sharp eye when she is faced with a handsome suitor?" he demanded; and his glance was merry. "How can an eye be sharp when it is downcast?"

Mouse Woman's small nose twitched again. "Her eyes won't stay downcast after the marriage," she pointed out. "She'll see you put on your supernatural garment and turn into a bear. And she'll be horrified."

"Why should she be horrified? Don't these humans admire animals so much that they even call themselves Bears and Frogs and Wolves and Killer Whales and Eagles and Ravens?" he asked reasonably. "And, in any case, as soon as she eats our special food, she'll start turning into what I am."

What he was was a supernatural being whose spirit self could animate either of two shapes: bear or human; or it could dart around the world without any body.

"But if she is careful not to eat your special food?" Mouse Woman suggested.

"Why should she be careful? She wouldn't know it was special."

"She would if I told her," Mouse Woman said. And her nose twitched three times.

"Why would you tell her and make her unhappy with her lot as my wife?" he demanded to know; and he scowled at the Place's busiest busybody. "Is she happy as she is?"

"Well . . ." Mouse Woman hedged. The princess, Rh-pi-sunt, was not a joyous girl. In fact, Mouse Woman admitted to herself, Rh-pi-sunt was a spoiled, pampered, petulant, good-for-nothing babbler. Which made her strangely appealing to the little old narnauk. For to have a girl so lovely outside and so nasty inside did seem to make things equal. Yet it bothered Mouse Woman that Rh-pi-sunt was a girl who had been given a great name without being given the obligation that made things really equal, and so really satisfying. She pursed her lips severely.

Catching the thought that went with the pursed lips, Prince-of-Bears said, "She's exactly the kind of human to bring down the wrath of the bears on her village—if those boastful bear-hunting brothers of hers don't bring it down first. Think of it that way, Grandmother. By carrying her off, I'd be ridding her village of a source of trouble."

Mouse Woman narrowed her eyes on the handsome young man (keeping them firmly off his enticing woolen earbobs). "Since you know Rh-pisunt for what she is, my dear, why do you want to marry her?"

"Well . . ." He smiled disarmingly at the little old woman. "She is the most beautiful girl I have ever seen. And you know how fond I am of beautiful women." He chucked her under the chin.

Mouse Woman shook his hand off, though she did settle her field mouse robe more flatteringly on her shoulders. She regarded him severely.

"Perhaps I think she will change, when she understands," he said, in answer to the look. He, too, had been given a great name. But he had always understood the obligation that went with it to keep things equal. And that obligation now rang in his voice. "Grandmother, the happiness of the bears is in my hands. And it is threatened by the overweening pride of one family, who should be punished."

"By marriage to *you*," Mouse Woman said slyly. (And she poked one woolen ear ornament and set it swinging.)

"Yes, since capture is shame to the proud ones," he said, ignoring her little joke.

Mouse Woman nodded. So much she agreed with. The bad should be punished. The arrogant should be humbled. "But marriage between a human and a supernatural being?"

"Nothing else will do," he assured her. "When I have married Rh-pi-sunt and we have had a child, the bears will begin to regard those humans as their relatives; while those humans will begin to wonder, every time they see a bear, if *he* is one of *their* relatives. And it will make each side hesitate to harm the other." For blood kinship was sacred in the vast green wildernesses of the Northwest.

Mouse Woman nodded. And her shoulders sagged in defeat.

Or was she defeated? Suddenly her shoulders squared; her nose twitched; her eyes flashed with purpose. "We shall see, my dear. For it will not be a proper marriage." (She poked all his earbobs, in turn, and set them tangling.)

"We shall see," he agreed. Then he moved off.

Mouse Woman sighed. She would have loved to take those woolen ear ornaments in her fingers and ravel them into a lovely, loose, nesty pile of mountain sheep wool. She couldn't wear such ornaments herself. Nor a handsome woolen robe. Because of her ravelly fingers.

Then she transformed herself into a white mouse, scampered down the rock, and scurried off to watch the Trail.

Since nothing ever escaped her sharp eyes, she had made herself Guardian of the Trail-into-the-Place-of-Supernatural-Beings. It was a job that delighted her. It made everyone look up to the tiniest of narnauks. And that was strangely satisfying.

BECAUSE IT WAS the time of berries, Rh-pi-sunt's people were not at their winter village. They were camped at the end of a lake where ducks paddled among the water lilies, where songbirds warbled in the pale aspens along the lake and in the darker pines and spruce trees behind them, and where, at times, the still of the evening was broken by the wild laughter of a loon.

Hunters glanced eagerly at the hills where the bears roamed. But now the hunters were fishermen, taking salmon from the river. It was women who were climbing the hills with berry baskets slung on their backs by a tumpline, a carrying strap around the forehead.

One morning as the young women were about to start out for the hills, the Wolf princess, Rh-pi-sunt, strode out of her hut. Clearly she was in a black mood. For when her small dog Maesk almost tripped her, she toed it out of the way so vigor-

ously that it slunk off with her youngest brother.

"What am I supposed to do all day while the other girls are off picking berries?" she demanded of her mother.

"You could finish decorating your berry basket, my dear," her mother answered, smiling indulgently at her.

"Why?" Rh-pi-sunt wanted to know. "When do I go berry picking?"

"Perhaps you should go now, my dear. A great lady should be skilled. Your husband will expect it." Her daughter's lack of skill made the mother's eyes anxious.

"My husband!" the princess scoffed. "When will you find a young man you think good enough for me?"

"When indeed?" Her mother's eyes were a little anxious about that too. "But we will find one. So prepare yourself for your great position. Go with the girls, my dear."

The princess scowled at the lopsided berry basket that had refused to come out straight when she was making it. "It's not fit for a princess to carry." She looked accusingly at it.

"Then take this one." Her mother offered a beautiful basket.

"I don't want that one," the princess answered rudely. And she slung on her own badly made basket. "Wait for me!" she called out.

Instantly every young woman stopped where

she was. For by her birth, Rh-pi-sunt was a very
great lady. A long line of proud, skilled, gentle-
voiced noblewomen had worn the name Rh-pi-
sunt, giving it great luster.

"Oh, go on!" their spoiled descendent ordered.
"Just my two girls will stay with me."

Her two friends-and-attendants sighed, fetched
a light woolen robe for her possible comfort, and
resigned themselves to a bad day. The princess,
they knew, would *not* remember that these hills
were the home of the bears. She would not care
that berry pickers must sing as they moved along,
to alert the bears to their presence. For it angered
a bear to be suddenly surprised in his own berry
patches. And if the bear were a grizzly, his claws
could be murderous.

Yet their eyes softened as they looked at their
mistress. Rhi-pi-sunt was as beautiful as the
aspens, as stately as the spruce trees. Her hair hung
dark and glossy over bare shoulders, while the
elegantly decorated aprons of her breechclout
touched her graceful limbs lightly. Ear ornaments
—long woolen tassels weighted with squares of
abalone pearl—mingled with her dark hair. And
the slant eyes of Wolf glinted from her copper
necklace. But the princess's own eyes smouldered
with annoyance.

"Now don't remind me about the singing!" she
ordered her two girls. Every Rh-pi-sunt had sung
like a warbler-in-spring, she knew, while her own

song came out tuneless to her ears. So she did not intend to sing to please the bears. The big ugly brutes could stay out of her way without her help.

The three girls climbed up into the hills and began picking berries.

"Bears!" Rh-pi-sunt exclaimed, when she should have been singing. "The bears know who my brothers are." And for the benefit of any hovering bears, she launched into an account of how her eldest brother had once gone out and killed twenty bears. Then she told of how her second brother had once gone out and killed fifteen of the awkward brutes.

Her two friends hid their dismayed eyes from her while *they* kept on singing to alert the bears.

"Stupid old berries!" Rh-pi-sunt cried out as she rubbed a scratched arm. "Let the stupid bears have them!"

Then her badly-made tumpline broke. And her berries spilled on the trail.

"Leave them!" her friends urged her. "We have plenty to share with you." One dipped handsful of berries out of the good baskets while the other girl mended the broken tumpline. "There, my dear, you have plenty of berries."

But the princess angrily started to pick up her own spilled berries. So, of course, the two girls had to help her.

"Now do sing, my dear!" they urged her, when they once more started picking. "We really must not anger the bears, who provide us with food and warm robes."

"What do I care about the bears?" Rh-pi-sunt answered. And she went on to boast of how her third brother had once gone out and killed thirteen of the ugly brutes.

Then, right in the middle of her boast, she slipped on some bear dung and fell down.

"Ohhhhhhhh!" she screamed; and now she was furious, as well as hot and scratched and dirty. "That horrible beast put his stinking dung just where he knew I would slip on it." She began wiping her foot against a small log.

"We will clean your foot, my dear," one of the girls said, starting to sing again as she kneeled down to do it. The other girl also sang as she picked up spilled berries.

"Stupid bears!" Rh-pi-sunt said, louder than the singing. "Wait until my brothers hear what they did to me!"

"Sh! sh!" her friends begged the princess. And both started singing as loud as they could to drown out her offending words.

Then they all started picking once more. But the princess's tumpline broke, again! And as before her girls hurried to pick up her spilled berries and to mend her broken tumpline, singing all the while.

"Perhaps we should go back now," one of them suggested. "It's such a hot day. And we must not let you overtire yourself. Look, my dear! Many of the others are turning back now."

"Because their baskets are full. While mine is nearly empty." She looked accusingly at it.

"Have some of ours!" her girls offered, dipping quick hands into berry baskets.

"No!" I can pick as well as anyone else," the princess announced. "And I can do it better without you to keep me back with your silly chatter and your sillier singing." She wiped a hand across her hot face. "You go back!" she ordered.

"But—"

"Do as I tell you!" she almost screamed at them. "Must I always be plagued by your infuriating skill and your perfect patience and your utterly proper behavior?" Her eyes flashed with tears while her voice broke with fury. "Do as I tell you!" She stamped her foot. On a sharp twig. "Now look what you've done!" she yelled, hopping about in pain. "Do as I tell you and GO BACK!"

The two girls glanced at one another. And their eyes flashed. They were high ranking attendants and not slaves, as the princess seemed to think. And it was high time someone let the princess suffer a little. "Well," one of them said coldly, laying the light woolen robe on a log, "We could send someone back to help you."

"I can find my own way down the mountain," Rh-pi-sunt screeched at them, hopping about on her good foot. "Just GO!"

"Well . . . if you insist," the girls said, only too glad to go, but still anxious about their duty. And they went, singing rather nervously as they went. When Rh-pi-sunt was in one of her wild black moods, she was impossible. But they would send someone back to help her. After all, she was precious to the Wolf Clan. She carried the royal bloodline.

IT WAS NOT MUCH LATER, and Rh-pi-sunt's basket was not much fuller when she set it down and scowled at it from a seat on a log. Stupid old basket! It would probably break again and spill out all her berries, so that she would have to limp home with a miserable mess . . . which she would throw at the first person who said something about it.

"I came to help you, Princess."

Startled by the suddeness of the voice, Rh-pi-sunt sprang up. And one glance at the handsome young stranger made her realize that her own skin was all dirt and scratches and berry stains, her own hair was a tangle of leaves and small twigs; while her basket was a lopsided disgrace. She bristled to cover her confusion.

"I don't need help," she said, as haughtily as a princess could say anything when her skin was all dirt and scratches and berry stains, when her hair was a tangle of leaves and small twigs, and when her basket was a lopsided disgrace.

But she did need help. And she was so overcome
by the charm of the young man that—for a moment—she forgot herself.

He was taller and fairer than her brothers. And
a bearskin robe slung from one shoulder partly
hid the magnificent totem tattooed across his chest.
It was a Bear crest, she knew, but an unfamiliar
one; for of course she had never seen the supernatural Prince-of-Bears crest. It was his bearing
that told her it was a princely emblem.

Hope sprang up. Perhaps she could do what
her parents had failed to do—find a husband good
enough for her. Rh-pi-sunt's eyes flashed with
spite for her mother. And her voice turned as
sweet as honey.

"My berries are scarcely worth taking home,"
she said, to sweeten her first rude response to his
offer of help.

"Then we'll leave them for the bears," he said,
cheerfully moving them to the side of the trail.

"Of course!" she agreed, trying to appear more
generous than she was; for generosity was a great
virtue. "I'd love to leave them for the bears."

He picked up her light woolen robe and dropped
it around her shoulders; a breeze had sprung up
on the mountain, where the shadows were length-
ening.

Her girls must have met him on the trial, Rh-pi-
sunt thought. But why had they sent a stranger to
help their princess? She stole a glance at his fine

form and princely bearing. So charmed was she with the young man, and with her designs on him, that she failed to notice he was taking her gradually up the mountain, instead of back down toward the lake where her people were.

Then, suddenly, their way was blocked by a stand of wickedly thorny devil's club. But the young man only smiled and led her around to a hidden opening. And when they had glided through the thorny hedge, they stood on the edge of a cliff. Below them stretched an awesome valley, walled on all sides by towering cliffs. Yet there were houses in the valley.

Her eyes widened with a question. How could anyone get down into the valley?

He led her along the top of the cliff until, suddenly, there was a switchback trail down. A wide trail marvellously concealed by alpine trees and flowering bushes.

A squeak made her jump. A mouse looked out from under some leaves and then scurried back into the bushes.

"A *white* mouse?" she asked, startled.

"A white mouse," he agreed; and a frown darkened his face for an instant. "This is an unusual place."

It was a most unusual place. For, even before they had reached the valley floor, several very young bears were tumbling and wrestling around them, and flinging themselves at the young man.

Rh-pi-sunt shrank back. She did not like bears.

But the young man fondled them and scratched their bellies. He wiped off their tongue licks with obvious pleasure.

"Cubs are the most affectionate and joyous of young beings," he said, waving them away.

"But—" But Rh-pi-sunt closed her mouth on her petulant protest. For he was a very, very handsome young man.

"I've brought you to my village," he said. And he led her directly to the huge house in the center of the village. It was a house carved and painted with a strange variety of Bear crests.

At the entrance to the house he stopped. He hallooed brightly.

At once a voice answered from inside. "You have brought what you went for?"

"I have brought what I went for."

"Then bring her in that I may welcome my daughter-in-law."

"Daugh—" Rh-pi-sunt's mouth stayed open in amazement. He had brought her here to marry her? Without any family arrangements? Her! A very great princess! She bristled with indignation.

Then she noticed that the handsome young man was looking at her with something less than admiration. And suddenly she began to tremble. There was something strange and awesome about the house . . . about the whole valley . . . even about the young man.

He answered the voice of his father. "As soon as she has been made presentable, I will bring in your daughter-in-law." And with very little ceremony, he ushered her into the smaller house next door. He put her into the hands of two female slaves with a peremtory, "Clean up the princess!"

The slaves seated her on a mat by the fire, where bark coals were smouldering. And at once they began attending to skin that was all dirt and scratches and berry stains; they began combing hair that was a tangle of leaves and small twigs.

When they had finally gone off to report her readiness to someone in the big house, Rh-pi-sunt felt a tug at her robe. And there stood the tiniest old woman she had ever seen.

The strange little old grandmother had a field mouse robe, a twitchy nose, and big, busy, mouse eyes. She also had fingers that seemed to almost nibble at the princess's light woolen robe.

"Do you know who these people are?" she asked in a small squeaky voice.

Rh-pi-sunt swallowed.

"They are Bear People."

"Bear People?" Bear people were narnauks.

"Have you any goat fat?" the little being demanded. For of course she was Mouse Woman. And Mouse Woman did not give anything—even advice!—without receiving something in return. Especially from young people. For young people must be taught the obligation of a gift. Also they must be trained to be generous. Generosity was the great virtue.

Trembling now more than ever, the princess slipped a hand into her handbasket and drew out her cosmetic stick.

"Throw it into the fire!" There was a touch of impatience in Mouse Woman's voice. For young people should know that goat fat needed to be turned into its essence by fire before it could be used by spirit beings.

"Of course," Rh-pi-sunt answered, remembering her manners. This was a gift for a supernatural being. This was Mouse Woman, the one who often helped young people who had been carried off by a narnauk. The princess's hand trembled a little less as she threw the fat in the fire.

"You have woolen ear ornaments?" The big busy mouse eyes were searching the girl's head.

As if in a spell, Rh-pi-sunt took off her red tasseled earbobs and tossed them into the fire.

But before they were more than scorched, Mouse Woman darted forward and spirited them out of the coals. And her ravelly little fingers began tearing them into a lovely, loose, nesty pile of mountain sheep wool. Then, having received her favorite gift, she properly proceeded to give, in return, her favorite giving—advice to a young person who had been tricked into trouble.

"Do not eat any of the crabapples here," she told the princess. "Or you will turn into what they are."

"What . . . they are?" But Rh-pi-sunt knew what they were. They were Bear People. Supernatural beings whose spirit-self could animate either of two forms—bear or human—or could dart around the world without any body. Even HE was Bear People. She shuddered.

"He is Prince-of-Bears," Mouse Woman said; and she said it with some pride. "He has captured you because of your scorn for bears and because of your brothers' cruelty toward them."

Just then there were sounds of the slave women returning. Mouse Woman vanished.

And Rh-pi-sunt sat, trembling and alone by the smouldering bark coals. A captive of the mighty Bear People.

Her mind kept darting back to her rude scoffings in the berry patches, and to her boasts about her bear hunting brothers. Why hadn't her stupid girls *made* her sing? They were supposed to look after her, weren't they? For that matter, why had they left her all alone on the mountain? They should have known a narnauk would capture her.

Her anger helped her control her trembling while she was being taken into the big house where the young man's father waited to see his daughter-in-law.

The first thing she noticed in the big house was its carved posts and painted screens, all decorated in Bear crests. Then she noticed the many bear-skins hanging along the walls. And she swallowed. Were those the supernatural garments that trans-

formed human shapes into snuffling, lumbering bears? Finally she looked toward the great chief sitting beyond the fire, watching her.

This was the high chief of all the Bear People? Of the now-angered Bear People? Terror, rather than maidenly shyness, kept her eyes downcast as she approached him.

"Welcome, daughter-in-law!" he said in a gruff voice. And his head seemed to sway in a strange way. "You will sit here." He indicated one of the two elegantly woven cedar mats that had been placed near him.

She was in his power. There was nothing she could do to stop the horrifying marriage. So the princess swallowed again, and sat down.

Instantly the two female slaves brought a gorgeously soft white wolf fur robe to replace her own light woolen one.

She caught her breath. Why had slaves performed this marriage rite? Was she to be a slave wife? It was rumored that the Bear People always made slaves of their captives. Perhaps these very slaves attending her had once been free people. Rh-pi-sunt hugged her new fur blanket around her to stop her trembling.

She heard the approach of Prince-of-Bears.

"Sit down beside your bride," his father said, indicating the other elegantly woven cedar mat.

The handsome young man sat down beside Rh-pi-sunt, thereby accepting her as his bride. And he *was* handsome. The princess caught her breath, stealing a glance at him. If only he weren't a nar-nauk! If only he wouldn't put on a supernatural garment, one of these days, and become a shaggy, snuffling, lumbering bear with paws that cuffed rotting salmon out of a spawning stream! She shuddered, thinking of what would be.

"Now present my children with their food!" the great chief ordered.

At once slaves came, bearing beautifully carved bowls.

The princess noticed crabapples in the first bowl. And she shook her head.

Do not eat any of the crabapples here, Mouse Woman had advised her. *Or you will turn into what they are.*

Rh-pi-sunt looked pleadingly at the young man beside her. "I never eat crabapples," she lied, in a whisper.

His eyes narrowed on her. But the bowl of crab-apples was replaced by a bowl of steaming red salmon. And Rh-pi-sunt ate that.

Now she was the wife of Prince-of-Bears. As a punishment, she knew; for the eyes around her were hostile.

A rush of longing for her own dear pampering family filled her eyes with tears. But her pride blinked the tears back. She would not cry. Ever! And she would not eat their crabapples. Ever! And—somehow! sometime!—she would escape from the Bear People.

BACK AT HER PEOPLE'S CAMP, the ducks paddled among the water lilies; the songbirds warbled in the pale aspens along the lake and in the darker pines and spruce trees behind them; and the still of the evening was broken by the wild laughter of a loon.

The people started at the sound. For men were back from the salmon river. Women were back from the berry patches. But the Wolf princess had not returned.

"Why didn't you stay with your mistress?" her mother demanded of the two sobbing friends-and-attendants.

"She ordered us to leave her," they whimpered, as they had whimpered a dozen times. They were in deep trouble.

Trackers came back from the hills. "The princess moved off up the mountain," they reported, "but her tracks are lost under scuffles of bear tracks; and her scent is lost under sweepings of devil's club."

The princess had vanished.

"The bears have taken her," people whispered to one another. And their eyes glanced accusingly at her boastful bear-hunting brothers. "Tomorrow we will find her mauled body." For bears did not eat people.

For several days they searched the hills. But they did not find her mauled body. "So," people whispered, "perhaps the bears have not taken her.

Perhaps a narnauk has taken the princess."

Her father turned to the shaman, the witch-doctor. "Find out where she is!" he ordered; but he ordered it with great respect. For a shaman had power to harm as well as to help people. "Find out where my daughter is!"

The shaman put on a dancing apron that clattered with a fringe of bird beaks. He put a crown of grizzly bear claws over his long straggly gray hair. He picked up his medicine rattle and his white eagle tail feather. Then, as the cedar drums boomed out over the lake, he began to circle the fire in a wild leaping dance. The dance grew faster and wilder, faster and wilder, faster and wilder until, suddenly, the shaman collapsed onto a tattered wolf robe that had been readied for him. And he lay as though dead.

The people hushed themselves. For the shaman's spirit-self had now left its body to make a spirit journey in search of the princess. They waited, almost holding their breath.

At long, long last, the shaman seemed to stir. And the people began to chant softly, luring his spirit-self back to its body.

"I saw the princess," he announced, sitting up. And his eyes were the wild, glittering eyes of one who has seen things that mortal men do not see.

People held themselves hushed to hear him.

"The Bear People hold her captive."

"The Bear People!" Her relatives shrank back.

For the Bear People were narnauks who made *slaves* of their captives.

Her three outraged eldest brothers strode off, their faces dark with anger. For captivity was a deep disgrace. It was a shame that would have to be lifted from the family. "The bears will pay for this," they muttered to one another. And day after day after day they hunted the hills mercilessly.

Even after the people had moved back to their winter village, the three brothers continued to hunt the hills, searching for bears as well as for their sister. And people turned alarmed eyes on the bear meat the brothers threw down before them, and on the bearskins the brothers dragged on the ground, with no respect for the bears who had worn them. For it would be a terrible thing to anger the bears so much that they would leave the mountain. Forever!

Then the thunder rolled. The snow fell on the mountain. And people knew the bears would be going into their dens to sleep.

"Now we can smoke them all out and kill them!" the eldest brother boasted.

"Or smoke them all to death in their dens," the second and third brothers agreed.

"But . . . what if our sister is in a bear's den?" the youngest brother asked, fondling little Maesk's head.

His three older brothers narrowed their eyes. Then they asked the shaman to see if their sister was still in the house of the Bear People.

The shaman put on his dancing apron that clattered with bird beaks. He put his crown of grizzly bear claws over his long straggly gray hair. He picked up his medicine rattle and his white eagle tail feather. Then, as the clappers clacked, and the plank drums thudded hypnotically through the big windowless house, he began to circle the fire in a wild leaping dance. The dance grew faster and wilder, faster and wilder, faster and wilder until, suddenly, the shaman collapsed onto the tattered wolf robe that had been readied for him. And he lay as though dead.

The people hushed themselves. For the shaman's spirit-self had again left its body to make a spirit journey in search of the princess. They waited, almost holding their breath.

At long, long last he seemed to stir. So the people began to chant softly, luring his spirit-self back to its body.

"The princess is still in the house of the Bear People," he announced, sitting up.

So the eldest brother took his climbing staff and his snowshoes that were spiked with mountain goat horntips. He went off with his hunters and his slaves. And, after a moon, he returned with the skins of sixty bears.

"Sixty!" people said, aghast at such a slaughter. But they stifled their protests. For they understood that the princess's shame could be lifted only at a great potlatch where throngs of people would have to be fed, and where scores of chiefs would have to be given rich gifts.

Then, after once more consulting the shaman, the second brother went off with his climbing staff and his snowshoes, his hunters and his slaves. And, after a moon, he returned with the skins of forty bears.

"Forty!" people said, aghast at such a slaughter. But again they stifled their protests.

Then, after once more consulting the shaman, the third brother went off with his climbing staff and his snowshoes, his hunters and his slaves. And, after a moon, he returned with the skins of twenty bears.

"Twenty!" people said, aghast at such a slaughter. And now their protests were not stifled. The brothers had failed to find their sister. And the wanton slaughter might anger the bears so much that they would leave the mountain forever!

The brothers strode angrily through the village, ignoring the mutters and the anxious faces.

"Now I will go," their youngest brother announced, after once more consulting the shaman.

"You?" the other three scoffed. For their youngest brother was a mere boy. And he had no skill in hunting. In fact, when he should have been developing his hunting skills, he had been roaming the hills talking to all the animals as if *they* were his brothers.

"I will find our sister," the youngest brother insisted.

"But—What hunters? . . ." What hunters would go with such a boy?

"I will go without hunters, and without slaves," the youngest brother announced. "Just Maesk will go with me."

"Maesk?" A pet dog! A princess's pet dog!

"Maesk and I will find her," the youngest brother assured them. And he went off with his climbing staff and his snowshoes. He carried food, a fur blanket, and a hunting knife. His father had insisted that he take the knife.

As THE SHAMAN had seen in his spirit journey, the princess was, indeed, still in the house of the Bear People, in the Place-of-Supernatural-Beings, high in the mountains. But her husband planned to move her to a bears' den. For the princess was to be a mother.

"My child must be born in a bears' den," Prince-of-Bears told her. It was the sacred custom.

"But—A bears' den!" Rh-pi-sunt said, horrified. A great princess should not have her child in a bears' den. And she almost burst into tears before she remembered that she would *not* cry. During all the moons in the Place, she had never cried. And she had never, never eaten their crabapples.

She watched her handsome husband take his supernatural garments off the wall. Then she turned her head away. For she would *not* see him become a shaggy, snuffling, lumbering bear with paws that could cuff rotting salmon out of a spawning stream. She could be fond of a handsome young man. But a bear! She shuddered at the very thought.

"I should think you would turn your head away from a bear," he said; and his voice was as cold as the wind from an ice field. "Turn it away in shame."

Rh-pi-sunt did not answer. She knew that her eldest brother had killed sixty of the bears, without proper respect for their spirit-selves. She knew her second brother had killed forty of the bears, also without respect. And her third brother had killed twenty.

The killings and the manner of the killings had angered her husband. But he had not taken revenge on the brothers. "They're my brothers-in-law," he had moaned. And kinship was sacred in the vast green wildernesses.

The other Bear People had nodded in understanding. Even when tears of sorrow were trickling down their noses, they had nodded in understanding.

"We must be patient," Prince-of-Bears reminded them.

And they had understood that, too. For his child would be the sacred tie of kinship joining those merciless brothers to the bears they hunted.

Now he said, "My child must be born in a bears' den." Then his voice turned hard as an icicle as he added, "When I return, I will give you the choice of three dens."

She heard him pad out on his bear paws.

"The choice of three dens," Rh-pi-sunt whispered in dismay.

She felt a tug at her robe. And there stood Mouse Woman.

"You have woolen ear ornaments?" the tiny grandmother asked; though her big, busy, mouse eyes were watching the blue and green earbobs.

The princess took them off and tossed them onto the very edge of the smouldering bark coals.

Mouse Woman pulled them out. And her ravelly little fingers began tearing them into a lovely, loose, nesty pile of mountain sheep wool. Then, having received her favorite gift, she proceeded to give, in return, her favorite giving— advice to a young person who had been tricked into trouble.

"When your husband gives you the choice of three dens, my dear, choose the Den-With-Slides-on-Both-Sides. It is near your own village, so your youngest brother will easily reach it."

"My youngest brother?" A rush of longing for her favorite brother so overwhelmed Rh-pi-sunt that she almost wept.

"Your youngest brother and Maesk are now searching for you."

"Maesk!" Her little pet dog. Rh-pi-sunt blinked hard to keep the tears back. "Oh, I will indeed choose the Den-With-Slides-on-Both-Sides, Grandmother," she said. "And I will watch for my brother."

But Mouse Woman had vanished.

The princess hugged her fur robe about herself and the child she would bear. And now her eyes glinted with purpose. She would not have her child in a bears' den! Her youngest brother and Maesk would find her. She would escape to her own village. And she would have her child as a great princess should have her child. In a beautiful carved cedar house.

It was a long time before her husband returned. Then, once more a handsome young man, he gave her the choice of three dens. "Will our child be born in the Den-of-the-Steep-Slope? Or the Den-of-the-High-Peak? Or the Den-with-Slides-on-Both-Sides?"

The princess appeared to consider, though her heart was pounding. Then she said—as though still a bit uncertain—"I choose the . . . the Den-with-Slides-on-Both-Sides."

His eyes narrowed on her. Then they glanced about, as if searching for a white mouse. "Our child will be born in the Den-with-Slides-on-Both-Sides," he agreed. But his voice had turned sad.

It was a long, weary, snowshoe trip through the

mountains, with a need to camp along the way. It was such a long, weary, snowshoe trip that often the handsome young man picked up his wife and carried her in his arms. He was tireless. When they arrived at the Den-with-Slides-on-Both-Sides, he was as fresh as when they had started. And he cheerfully started a fire, roasted a dried salmon, and made a comfortable bed of fur robes for the weary princess.

Rh-pi-sunt felt a rush of tenderness toward him. But she stifled the feeling. For she was going to escape from him. For ever and ever and ever!

Once he had her settled comfortably in the den, Prince-of-Bears went out daily for firewood, leaving the princess alone.

Alone. And alert. For she was watching for her youngest brother and for her dog, Maesk. But before they had appeared, she knew that her child was about to be born. He would be born in a bears' den after all, as her husband had intended. Yet the child would not remain in the den, but would be taken to her village. She was determined.

Prince-of-Bears came back with the firewood. The child was born. Twins.

Twins! Twin balls of dark fur!

They were BEAR CUBS.

"My children?" Rh-pi-sunt cried out, horrified.

"And mine," their father said, holding the cubs close. He touched their little black noses fondly. He scratched their tiny bellies.

"Remember that small bears are the most affectionate and joyous of children," he told the princess. Though now his eyes were anxious, for all children needed a fond mother.

But Rh-pi-sunt shrank away from her children.

Sadly Prince-of-Bears took off their tiny supernatural garments, revealing twin boys. And in their human form, he handed them to their mother.

The helplessness of human babies overcame the shock and endeared them to their mother. But dismay lingered in her dark eyes.

A week went by. The boy and the dog still did not come. And the twin boys had become alarmingly different from human babies. At one week, they were tumbling about the cave, bumping into one another; they were staggering from one parent to the other to be fondled. Like bear cubs.

Then, early one morning, Rh-pi-sunt thought she heard a dog bark. Thankful that her husband had left for more firewood, she darted out of the den. She scanned the slopes. And she called out, clearly but softly, "Maesk? Maesk?"

And Maesk, standing on a ledge halfway up the slope, started wildly barking and wagging his tail. He glanced back at his master, who was bogged down far below him.

Softened with springtime, the snow kept sliding beneath the boy's snowshoes. He had not heard his sister, but he had determined to see why Maesk was barking and wagging his tail.

Throbbing with joy, yet yearning over the weariness of her young brother, Rh-pi-sunt watched him struggle up to the spot where Maesk waited. But when he had finally reached the ledge, he was too weary even to glance up. He just flung himself down, exhausted.

She knew he had not seen her. So Rh-pi-sunt took a handful of snow and packed it hard with her fingers. Then she tossed her snowball gently down the slope, landing it near the tip of her brother's snowshoe.

He picked up the snowball, saw the marks of her fingers, and leaped up. Catching sight of her at last, he started on up the slope . . . climbing . . . slipping back . . . climbing . . . slipping back again . . . and climbing on with dogged determination.

And now her heart really pounded. If only he reached the top in time for her to hide him and Maesk far back in the den for the night, ready for escape in the morning, after her husband had left for more firewood!

The boy was almost at the top when Prince-of-Bears arrived.

The princess swallowed in dismay.

The handsome young man's eyes glinted with anger. Then they softened with compassion as he watched the boy's struggle to reach his sister.

"Welcome, brother-in-law," he said, reaching out a strong hand to help him up the last bit.

Rh-pi-sunt's arms engulfed her brother. And—
at long, long last!—she wept. She wept for sorrow as well as for joy, for herself as well as for
him. For how could she escape now? With her husband there beside her.

Prince-of-Bears vanished into the den. And in
a moment he reappeared, wearing his bear shape.
The princess gasped. And her brother's mouth
opened in amazement.

It opened even wider when the bear spoke, in
the man's voice. "You must kill me," the bear said.

"Kill . . . you?" The boy was dismayed. He
had never killed even a salmon. How could he kill
a bear who was his brother-in-law?

"You must kill me," Prince-of-Bears repeated.

"You must do as he says," Rh-pi-sunt told her
brother, though she felt tears running down her
face.

Aghast at what he must do, the boy took out
his hunting knife. He looked at it with horror.

"You must kill me," Prince-of-Bears insisted.

Somehow, the boy lifted the knife. Somehow,
he plunged it into the bear, who fell with a mighty
thud.

Before either the princess or her brother could
recover from the shock of the killing, the handsome young man stood with them, looking at the
bear carcass. For, of course, his spirit-self had not
died. It had simply taken on its other—its human
—shape.

"Now," he said sternly, turning toward them. "Now you must sing the bear's dirge." He sang the dirge over and over and over, until they could sing it with him.

Then Prince-of-Bears gave a command to his young brother-in-law. "Now you must take this red ochre and paint a line on the bear's body. From his head to his tail."

With tears of genuine remorse streaming from his eyes, the boy drew the red line.

"When the bear dies at your hand, he gives you food and fur," Prince-of-Bears reminded the boy. "And what do you give in return? . . . You give him the reverence that nourishes his spirit-self, so that it will come back to the mountain again, to nourish you again. The obligation of a gift is the great law that keeps all things equal in the world. This you must tell the people . . . And as a reminder, forever, you must show this to the people." He gave the boy a bone charm carved with the Prince-of-Bears Crest. "This is a new crest for you and for your descendents. A crest to remind them, forever, of their obligation to the bears who give them food and comfort."

Then Prince-of-Bears led the boy into the den so that his sister could warm him with food and fire and thick fur robes.

The twin boys looked at their uncle with bright black eyes. They flung themselves on him to be fondled. And the boy hugged them.

In the morning, the bear carcass was gone.

Without a word, the handsome young man wrapped his small sons warmly in bearskins. He tucked them carefully into a moss bag, which he placed on his wife's back, with the tumpline around her forehead. "You will leave me now," he told the tiny boys. "But you will come back to me, when the time comes." He patted their little heads fondly. Then, still without a word to the princess, he vanished. As if he had never been, he vanished.

Rh-pi-sunt blinked back a rush of tears. And she was almost blinded by tears as she followed her young brother away from the bears' den, away toward their village. Her husband was gone from her, forever. Yet, as she travelled over the snow, it was as if a strong arm held the moss bag so that she felt no weight on her forehead. It was as if a strong arm lifted her, too, so that her snowshoes almost flew over the softening snow.

Then they were down in the valley, where the trees were leafing.

They were nearing their village. And relatives were streaming out to welcome the vanished princess and the brother who had found her.

People's eyes widened at sight of the moss bag. They opened wider yet when the tiny boys were lifted out. For the infants began tumbling over one another. They began bumping into one another, and also into other people.

"They're like bear cubs," the princess's father murmured. "The most affectionate and joyous of children." He hugged his strange grandsons; and they clung boisterously to him.

Their grandmother did not touch them. In fact, she shrank away from them. She was clearly aghast at the nature of the twin boys, who were indeed like bear cubs. And as the days and the weeks passed, she still kept her distance from them.

Yet, now and then, the boisterous boys bumped into her as they romped.

Always, she glared at them. Not only were they bear cubs in her eyes, they were also slave children. For Rh-pi-sunt had been captured by the Bear People, hadn't she? And Bear People were known to make slaves of their captives. The once-indulgent mother looked askance at her daughter.

The princess was indeed in disgrace. For had she not become a slave?

Her family gave a great potlatch feast to lift the shame from her. But at the potlatch they took away her proud name. For Rh-pi-sunt was a title to be worn only by the unblemished. With much ceremony, they bestowed it on the princess who was next-in-line to the shamed one, the daughter of her mother's sister. For the younger girl was now a more proper princess to carry the royal bloodline.

With her pride shattered, the young mother

held herself back in the corners of the big house. She slipped off into the woods alone—especially during the times when her little sons disappeared. She knew they went to see their father, who was probably hovering near the village. Being supernatural like him, they heard his voice in the silence, calling them. And they rushed off with joy.

But they always came back to her. And as the moons passed, they grew even more boisterous. To the consternation of the people, they started climbing up the house posts and the totem poles with merry disregard for the proud crests that were carved there.

"Make a play pole for my grandsons!" the chief ordered.

A carver made a pole with one bear figure at the top and one at the bottom. And the boys loved to climb it.

"The Play-Pole-of-the-Bears," people dubbed it, smiling at the twins' antics, yet not quite daring to chuckle. For clearly the boys were narnauks.

One day, a year or so later, when they were especially boisterous, the twins bumped into their grandmother and knocked that great lady over.

"Slaves!" she screamed at them. "Sons of a slave-wife!"

The boys looked up at her with dismay. And tears ran down their faces as they ran to their mother.

"The time has come," she said to them sadly,

"as your father said it would come."

They glanced eagerly toward the hills. And their eyes were alert, as if they heard something. Then, as one, they bounded off to the mountains, tumbling and wrestling like two joyous bear cubs.

Their mother watched them go. And her eyes were sad. She walked swiftly toward the woods, where no one could see the once-proud princess weeping. From now on her life would be sad and lonely. From now on, she would always be yearning for what-might-have-been.

ALONG THE TRAIL, the handsome young man was waiting for his sons, waiting with their supernatural garments.

They threw themselves on him in an ecstacy of fondness. Then they almost held still while he put on their bearskins. And in a few minutes they were tumbling and wrestling and cuffing one another, now truly two joyous and boisterous young bears.

Suddenly they saw a white mouse. And with the quickness of young bears, they snatched it up and began tossing it to one another. Though it squeaked its outrage.

A word from their amused father made them place the white mouse on a high rock, where it turned instantly into the tiniest and most furious of little old women.

"You deserved that, Grandmother," the handsome young man told her. "For interfering."

She settled her field mouse robe on her tiny shoulders. "It was not a proper marriage," she countered.

"It might have been," he told her, "if you hadn't been such a busybody."

"If I hadn't been such a busybody," she retorted, "you would not have gained what you wanted." (And her big, busy, mouse eyes began watching his brown woolen ear ornaments.)

"I lost what I wanted," he retorted in turn.

"And so gained what you really wanted," she assured him with much satisfaction. (And she poked one woolen earbob in triumph.) "For now the people will keep wondering about those two young rascals." She nodded toward the young bears. (Then her eyes once more began coveting the woolen earbobs.)

The handsome young man placed his hands over them. "Since we did deprive you of your dignity, if only briefly, Grandmother," he said, "I suppose it is only proper to compensate you." He took off his ear ornaments and handed them to her.

"It is only proper," she agreed. And her ravelly little fingers began tearing them into a lovely, loose, nesty pile of mountain sheep wool.

Then she vanished.

BUT WHAT she had said was true.

The people of the village did begin to wonder about those two young rascals. More and more as the years passed, the hunters wondered—each time they saw a bear—if *he* was one of *their* relatives. And they remembered what Prince-of-Bears had said to the princess's brother.

So it was that, when they had killed a bear for need, they sensed his spirit-self standing there watching them as Prince-of-Bears had stood watching the boy. And they sang the bear dirge. They drew the red line along the bearskin from head to tail. In return for the fur and food the bear had provided, they nourished his spirit-self with proper reverence, so that it would come back to the mountains again. For truly, they saw, honoring the obligation of a gift was the only way to keep things right in the world. To give was the only way to get. Generosity was the great virtue.

As more years passed, storytellers told and re-told the story of the vanished princess who had become the Bear Mother. Carvers began making images of the beautiful young mother and her bear cubs. And at the great potlatch feasts, young dancers put on their bear masks and dancing blankets to dance the tumbling, wrestling, cuffing, climbing, bumping-into-things dance of the most affectionate and joyous of children.

And sometimes when the dance ended, a white mouse circled the fire in a scurrying, merry little dance. For Mouse Woman found it strangely satisfying that the princess who had mocked the bears should be remembered forever as the Bear Mother.

3

The Princess and the Magic Plume

IT WAS IN THE TIME of very long ago, when things were different in the vast green wildernesses of the Northwest.

The totem pole village was nearer than its people knew to the Place-of-Supernatural-Beings.

And its Raven princess, Sagabin, had not really vanished. She had merely vanished from the everyday life of the village. Tribal puberty rites had banished her to a small compartment in a corner of her father's big cedar house. In fact, because of what happened later, Sagabin could be called the Princess-Who-Had-Not-Vanished-But-Probably-Wished-She-Had.

This is the way it happened.

THE YOUNG PEOPLE of the village became so rowdy that old people shook their heads and said it was too bad they couldn't *all* be banished to small separate compartments in big cedar houses across the mountain, or over the sea in the Haida Islands, or even under the sea in the fearsome dens of the devilfishes.

Late in the pale summer evenings, when their elders wanted to sleep, the young people were out there in the open space behind the village. They were wrestling and shouting, or climbing trees and shouting, or playing toss-the-kelp-holdfast and shouting, or even just shouting.

They knew they were annoying a lot of people in the village.

What they didn't know was that they were also annoying a lot of people in the Place-of-Supernatural-Beings. And those people were narnauks.

BEING NARNAUKS, the people in the Place-of-Supernatural-Beings could hear and see everything that was going on for leagues around. And they didn't like what was going on in that village. So they called a meeting.

In their human shapes, the Beings circled a fire for a powwow. And, like proper people, they had their Talking Stick handy. (The Talking Stick was the symbol of the right-to-speak. Whoever pounded it four times on the ground could speak to the powwow.)

"What are we going to do about those rowdy young people?" the powwow chief asked, holding the Talking Stick. And if his voice was gruff, it was merely because his mouth was as big as a berry basket.

"Well . . ." Mouse Woman squeaked, properly touching the Stick, though she was too small to pound it. "You all know that I'm very good at handling young people. I don't *tell* them what to do. I simply point out the dangers and let them have some choice in the matter. So perhaps I could talk to them and—"

The powwow chief cut her off. "In all that racket, Grandmother, they'd never even hear that squeak of yours."

Mouse Woman's nose twitched. She settled her fieldmouse robe on her tiny shoulders and sat down. But her ravelly little fingers were itching at the thought of all the woolen ear ornaments her solution might have given her.

"What about letting me handle it?" the Wild Woman of the Woods suggested. After all, she pointed out, she had an immense basket to put children into; she had pitch to gum up their eyes; and she had a hut in the woods where she could eat them.

"No! No! No!" Mouse Woman squeaked, scurrying up to touch the Stick. "That's no way to handle young people."

One of the Bird People came forward, a red-headed young man. He jerked his head this way and that to catch everyone's eye. Then he pounded the Talking Stick four times on the ground. "What about using the Live-Tree-of-Odors?" he suggested.

There was a buzz of agreement. For the Live-Tree-of-Odors could be spirited to any place. It could lure victims in by its fragrance. Then it could embrace them until their shouting days were over. It was a most affectionate—if permanent!—way of handling troublesome children.

But one of the Squirrel People, a young woman, took the Talking Stick from the young man. The last time they had used the Live-Tree-of-Odors, she reminded everybody, an unreasonable relative of the victim had slashed at its roots, cutting its power considerably.

Shoulders sagged. What *were* they going to do to stop that infuriating racket? A few of the Beings looked hopefully at Raven, the great and greedy Prince of Tricksters. But that huge man's eyelids were closed over his wicked black eyes. Since this project offered no great hope of food, he was clearly not interested.

So one of the Wolf People—a long, lean man with big teeth and slant eyes—took the Talking Stick and suggested Guldani. And again there was a buzz of agreement. For Guldani was a living arrow with a snake's head. It could be sent out after anyone. It never missed its target. And it had no roots to slash.

Mouse Woman leaped up and touched the stick,

which the Wolf Man pounded for her. "No! No! No!" she squeaked. "We are dealing with young people whose *parents* have failed to teach them the proper way to behave. So all your suggestions are too deadly."

"Deadly?" Raven's wicked black eyes opened. And no Stick was needed to make anyone listen to the great and greedy Prince of Tricksters. "Not too deadly, Grandmother. Just too deadly dull and serious."

People looked startled, then wildly hopeful. If Raven took over the project, things were sure to be lively.

But Mouse Woman had not yet taken her hand off the Talking Stick; so it was proper for *her* to do the talking. Her nose twitched and her big, busy, mouse eyes glared at Raven. "I always advise my young people," she went on, just as if no one had interrupted. "I let them choose what to do. You must let them have a choice!"

"Do I not always give my victims a choice?" Raven scoffed. "I pride myself on it. That's why I never have to feel guilty. My victims always do themselves in through their own foolishness. In fact, letting them feel free to choose is the secret of handling troublesome people."

"Especially when they are troublesome only because they are keeping you from the food you crave," Mouse Woman retorted, clinging firmly to the Talking Stick in defiance of his improper behavior. Then, with dignity, she settled her field mouse robe on her tiny shoulders and sat down.

Raven had taken over.

The young people would be cured of their shouting. Of course they might also be cured of their breathing at the same time. Everyone realized that. Still, if anybody could, Raven would stop that infuriating racket.

What did he have in mind? Every eye was on him.

"The Magic Plume," he said lazily. "What else?"

People opened their mouths to say, "Now, why didn't I think of that?" But they didn't say it. They just kept their mouths open. The Magic Plume. Of course!

Mouse Woman's nose twitched. Her eyes narrowed. They were going to let Raven handle the matter. And then proper behavior would demand that she not interfere.

A buzz of excitement was circling the fire, with nobody bothering about the Talking Stick. "The Magic Plume. Of course!" people were saying to one another. It would float down over the shouting children. And of course they would touch it. As Raven had said, their own foolishness would do them in. Mouse Woman had been right, too. Young people should be given a choice. Those rowdy, shouting, infuriating, ill-mannered children should feel free to touch or not to touch the huge, beautiful, sparkling, enticing rainbow feather that would float down from the sky as if it had fallen from a Heaven Bird. They kept glancing at clever Raven. But that arrogant Prince of Tricksters had his eyelids closed lazily over his wicked black eyes.

Mouse Woman glared at him. Certainly the infuriating racket would be stopped. But! There was something too simple about this. Too simple for Raven. He had something further in mind for the troublesome children.

"Well, Raven," she muttered to herself, "You're not the only one here with sharp eyes."

IT WAS EARLY in the pale summer evening. So the older people were still up and about in the village that was closer than they knew to the Place-of-Supernatural-Beings.

Except for the princess who had vanished into the small separate compartment in a corner of her father's house, all the young people were out in the open space behind the village. They were wrestling and shouting, or climbing trees and shouting, or playing toss-the-kelp-holdfast and shouting, or even just shouting.

Suddenly one of them screeched, "Look! Look! Look!" And she kept on screeching so shrilly that, one by one, the other children stopped their own screeching to see what on earth *she* was screeching about.

It was a feather. A huge, beautiful, sparkling, enticing rainbow feather. And it was floating down from the sky.

"It must have fallen from a Heaven Bird," a boy yelled. He started jumping to catch it.

"A Heaven Bird feather!" the others yelled. And they, too, started jumping to catch it.

The feather was floating down. But in such a tantalizing way! It would be almost within reach of the tallest jumper when a whiff of wind would waft it up and away. Then it would be almost within reach of another jumper when another whiff of wind would waft it up and away again. Then it would be almost within reach of yet another jumper when yet another whiff of wind would waft it up and away, yet again.

The new excitement in the young people's shouts and screeches made one parent after another go out and glance at the open space behind the village. But all they saw was the muddle of screeching jumpers.

"It's just some new game," they reported, one after another.

Then the screeches changed. For, suddenly, the tallest jumper caught the feather. And he waved it aloft—a huge, beautiful, sparkling, enticing rainbow feather.

"Catcher's keeper!" he yelled in triumph. And he put the huge, beautiful, sparkling, enticing rainbow feather into the hairknot on top of his head.

Instantly, he began to rise from the ground.

"It's caught HIM!" his friends cried out, aghast. And when his feet were on a level with his best friend's head, his best friend grabbed him by the ankles to pull him back to earth.

Only . . .

HE began lifting too. So his sister grabbed him by the ankles. And up SHE went. So her best friend grabbed her by the ankles. And up SHE went. So her brother grabbed her by the ankles. And up HE went.

The terrified screams of the rising young people brought their elders running. And the first father reached the spot just as the last child's feet were on a level with his head. So he grabbed the child by the ankles to pull him back to earth. And up HE went. So his wife grabbed him by the ankles. And up SHE went.

And so it went until fathers and mothers, uncles and aunts, grandfathers and grandmothers, and even young women with babies on their backs were rising up, up, up, up above the open space behind the village.

Only the princess was left in the village.

BANISHED INTO the small separate compartment in a corner of her father's house, Sagabin had heard all the lovely shouting in the open space behind the village. She had longed to be out there too, wrestling and shouting, or climbing trees and shouting, or playing toss-the-kelp-holdfast and shouting, or

even just shouting; though that would not have
been proper for the princess who carried the royal
bloodline.

She had heard the change in the screeching.
And she had been wild to know what was happening. In fact, she had (almost) hammered her
fists on the wall in a fury of frustration. But that
would not have been proper for the princess who
carried the royal bloodline.

Then she had heard the screams of alarm. She
had heard the rush of her elders toward the open
space behind the village. And she *had* hammered
her fists on the wall in a fury of frustration. What
on earth was happening?

Then she had heard the screams fading up, up,
up, up and away.

And now there was silence. A terrible silence.

Sagabin swallowed. Tribal rites did not permit
her to go out until her relatives came for her. If
she went out on her own, it would offend the
spirits; and something terrible would happen.

But!

What if something terrible had already happened? What if her relatives had vanished?

The silence was awesome. She shrank back
into her robe, hugging it about her.

Should she go out to see what had happened?

She felt a tug at her robe. And there was the
tiniest of old women, watching her with big, busy,
mouse eyes.

"Mouse Woman!" she gasped. Then she swallowed in dismay. For didn't Mouse Women appear to young people only when they were in deep distress? So something terrible *had* happened!

"You have woolen ear ornaments?" Mouse Woman asked, though her eyes were already coveting Sagabin's beautiful blue woolen tassels.

"Yes, Grandmother." Trembling with haste to show that her generosity made her worthy of help, the princess took them off and tossed them into the small fire that was taking the chill off the northern summer evening.

Mouse Woman darted forward to pull them out before they were more than scorched. And her ravelly little fingers began tearing them into a lovely, loose, nesty pile of mountain sheep wool. Then, having received her favorite gift, she properly proceeded to give her second-favorite giving —comfort to a young person in distress.

"All will soon be well again," she assured Sagabin. "The Magic Plume has merely carried off the young people because they were too noisy. It has carried off their elders too, because they allowed them to be so noisy," she explained. And her nose twitched. "They were disturbing everyone in the Place-of-Supernatural-Beings."

"Carried off?" The princess's eyes were wide with alarm. "Where to?"

"Oh . . ." Mouse Woman shrugged her tiny shoulders. "Just to some beach from which they can return, a chastened people."

But, at that very moment, there was a terrible thud-thud-thud-thud-thudding in the open space behind the village. And they both rushed out.

The princess screamed a scream that drowned out Mouse Woman's indignant little squeaks. For, instead of being carried off to some beach from which they could return, a chastened people, the villagers had been dropped back to earth. They had returned, not a chastened people, but a very dead people.

Sagabin sank to the ground, sobbing.

Mouse Woman danced up and down in fury. "This is not the proper way to use the Magic Plume," she raged. And if she had been a porcupine, she would have been shooting off quills. At Raven. For *he* had done this. He had cut across the power above the plume—a most improper thing to do.

But why had he done it? she asked herself.

"Hm," she answered herself. Raven was up to one of his tricks; and the trick was not yet over. Hadn't he said *their* ways of handling the troublesome young people were too deadly dull and serious? So he had something more entertaining in mind. In spite of the way it looked now, Raven would manage to make this a trick that people would laugh about forever in the feasthouses along the coast and along the rivers. Somehow, he would turn even this grisly act into a trick worthy of the great and greedy Prince of Tricksters.

"Greedy," she muttered. And she glanced at the houses which, she knew, would soon be the scene of his gluttonous orgy. But that would not be the end of it. Her nose twitched and twitched and twitched, thinking about it. Raven had something further in mind for the village of noisy children. But what could it be?

The princess was desolate.

"My dear," Mouse Woman comforted her. "The trick is not yet over."

Sagabin glanced up. "The trick?" she asked blankly.

"You will see, my dear," Mouse Woman cheered her.

Then she vanished.

The princess stayed where she was, sobbing.

By and by, she noticed a feather near the pile of very dead people. It was a huge, beautiful, sparkling, enticing rainbow feather. But she shrank away from it. "The Magic Plume," she murmured, shuddering. And without daring to touch it, she fled back to the house—the only one alive in the village that was closer than she knew to the Place-of-Supernatural-Beings.

She was all alone in the big, windowless house. All alone in a village of big, empty houses.

Then she caught her breath.

She was not alone.

All around her she sensed the ghosts of the dead

villagers. They were floating about her like drift-wood in a lake. Cold. Silent. And waiting . . . waiting . . . waiting . . .

For what?

Mouse Woman had said that the "trick" was not yet over.

So, terrified of what might happen next, Saga-bin huddled into a fur robe; she waited and waited for morning.

And all around her, the ghosts waited with her.

MOUSE WOMAN was back in the Place-of-Super-natural-Beings. And she was furious.

"That's no way to handle young people," she squeaked angrily to the huge dark man who was Raven in his human form.

"Grandmother!" he protested. "It's a very effec-tive way." His black eyes glittered. "The village is beautifully quiet this evening. And all the luscious food is free for the taking." He chucked her under the chin.

Mouse Woman shook off his hand. And she glared at him. "You can't leave a princess all alone in a village," she stormed. "It's not proper."

"Oh, my young friends will be joining her to-morrow morning," he said, lazily indicating the four young people who often hovered around the Prince-of-Tricksters.

Mouse Woman narrowed her eyes on those four imps; they had mischievous faces.

"Now, Grandmother!" Raven cautioned. "If you have any idea of poking your twitchy little nose into this affair, just remember that the pow-wow put it into my hands. So it's not proper for you to interfere."

"You're telling ME what's not proper?" she retorted. And she marched off with dignity. Defeated by the Prince-of-Tricksters.

Still . . .

There was nothing improper about keeping her big, busy, mouse eyes on the village of noisy-children-who-were-no-longer-noisy.

The princess might need a friend.

It was early the next morning when the princess emerged from her fur sleeping robe. She was hungry; but the house seemed strangely short of food.

Still hungry, she went out into the morning.

It was a strangely silent morning. No birds were chirping in the trees. No seagulls were wheeling and screaming above the beach. Even the usually raucous ravens were quiet at the edge of the forest.

Stilled by the ghosts?

Sagabin swallowed.

She could sense the ghosts still around her. The ghosts of the dead villagers. They were floating about her, like driftwood in a lake. Cold. And waiting. She sensed that they were still waiting . . . waiting . . . waiting . . .

For what?

Then she glanced over at the open space behind the village. And she caught her breath.

Overnight, the pile of dead people had turned into a pile of dead bones. It was as if the flesh had been spirited away, leaving only the white bones. The princess shuddered.

Then, suddenly, she sensed someone behind her. Terrified, she spun round. She looked into the faces of four young people—four young people with strangely mischievous faces.

"We have come to help you, Princess," the tallest of the four said.

Sagabin felt relief flooding through her. She was no longer alone with the ghosts, no longer alone with the big, empty houses, no longer alone with the horrible pile of bones. And she was so eager not to be alone again that she followed the four, even when they moved toward the open space behind the village.

She caught her breath when one of them picked up the feather—the huge, beautiful, sparkling, enticing rainbow feather. She waited for the girl to rise.

But nothing happened.

The girl with the feather glanced slyly at her friends. "Princess," she said, turning to Sagabin, "the Magic Plume can carry people off. But it can also bring them back again."

"Back from . . . ?" Sagabin could not say it.

"Yes. With our help," the girl assured her. And

she put the wonderful feather back on the ground again.

"Our help?" Sagabin almost sang it out, so eager was she to do anything that might bring the villagers back to the village. "What do we do?"

"Well . . ." the girl said, with another sly glance at her friends. "First we sort out the bones. Into separate people."

"Oh," Sagabin answered, shrinking back a little. "First we . . . sort out the bones . . . into . . . separate people?" Hesitantly she moved toward the pile. And even more hesitantly she picked up the first bone.

"Oh, we must do this quickly," the girl protested. "After all, the ghosts can wait around only so long. And a bone is a bone, Princess." She began to briskly sort out some bones and lay them in a separate pile. "Come on, Princess! Just take a main frame and be sure to add arm bones, leg bones, and a head for the top."

"Take a . . . main frame," Sagabin repeated, to be sure she had it right. "Then add arm bones, leg bones, and a head for the top."

"That's all there is to it," the girl assured her.

A squeak made them both jump. They glimpsed a flash of white. And the girl's eyes narrowed.

"Come on, everybody!" she urged. "We have to hurry." And more briskly than ever, she went to the task of taking a main frame and then adding arm bones, leg bones, and a head for the top. She put them into small piles.

Her friends, too, jumped into action, as briskly as she had. And soon the open space behind the village was almost as noisy as it had ever been with the clatter of bones and with young voices calling out, "Main frame, arm bones, leg bones, and a head for the top." "Main frame, arm bones, leg bones, and a head for the top." "Main frame, arm bones, leg bones, and a head for the top."

Sagabin worked a little less briskly. And she kept stopping. She kept hearing a squeak. She kept catching the flash of a white mouse.

Mouse Woman?

Was Mouse Woman impatient with her? With the slowness of her help? The princess tried to work faster. "A main frame, arm bones, leg bones, and a head for the top. . . . Main frame, arm bones, leg bones, and a head for the top."

But the white mouse kept on squeaking. It kept on flashing about. So Sagabin tried to work even faster.

At long last the clatter of bones and the cry of young voices stopped. The open space behind the village was covered with neat little piles of bones.

"And now . . . ?" the weary princess asked, looking anxiously at the main girl.

"And now!" the girl said triumphantly. "Now the Magic Plume brings them back to life." She picked up the huge, beautiful, sparkling, enticing

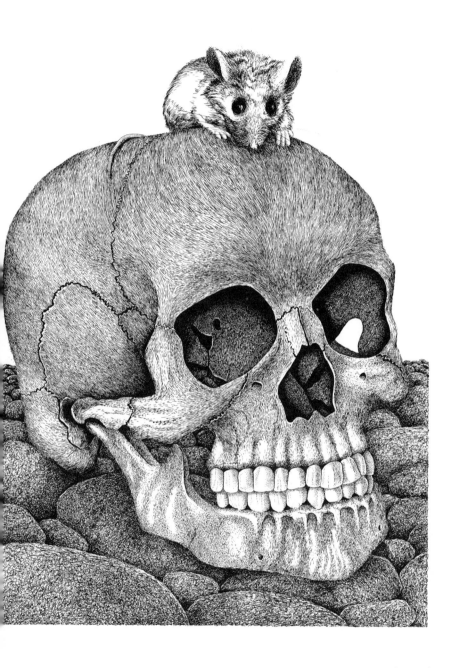

rainbow feather and held it out to the princess.

Sagabin heard the squeak. She saw the white mouse dart behind a pile of bones. And she hesitated.

Was it a warning?

What if the Plume carried her off, too? And dropped her back to earth, too?

But she had to try to bring back her relatives. So she took a deep breath, gritted her teeth, reached out, took the feather, shut her eyes, and waited. She waited for it to lift her.

But nothing happened.

"See, Princess!" the girl cried out in triumph. "Now! Wave the feather widely over the bones!"

Again Sagabin heard the squeak. *Was* it a warning? Again she hesitated. But she had to try to bring back her relatives, hadn't she? So she took a deep breath, gritted her teeth, shut her eyes, and waved the feather widely over the bones.

Instantly, there was a terrifying clatter. For all over the open space behind the village, each little pile was clattering its bones into their proper place, with its arm bones where they should be and the leg bones where they should be and the head at the top where it should be.

The clatter was terrifying. But at last it stopped. And the open space behind the village was a field of skeletons.

"Now, Princess!" the girl said, "Wave it widely again!"

Again there was the warning squeak. But what did it mean? She had to try to bring back her relatives, hadn't she? So Sagabin took a deep breath, gritted her teeth, shut her eyes, and waved the feather widely.

Instantly, the bones covered with flesh and skin. As if the flesh that had been spirited away during the night had now been spirited back, the bones looked like people again. But dead people.

"Now, Princess!" the girl cried out triumphantly. "Wave it once more!"

This time there was a babble of squeaks. The white mouse danced up and down, as if in a fury of frustration.

But—

Sagabin had to try to bring her relatives back to life, didn't she? So, one last time, she took a deep breath, gritted her teeth, and shut her eyes. Shutting her ears, too, to the frantic squeaks of warning, she waved the feather widely.

And if the white mouse was still sending out squeaks of protest, they were lost under a terrible rush of sound. It was like a wild rush of wind. Only it wasn't a rush of wind. It was the rush of all the ghosts back into their waiting bodies.

Alarmed by the sound, the princess opened her eyes. Then closed them again in a moment of thankfulness. For, all over the open space behind the village, people were stirring. They *were* coming back to life.

Only . . .

"Oh no!" Sagabin cried out. She sank to the ground in dismay. And this time she not only shut her eyes; she covered them with both hands. For everything was all wrong and mixed-up. A man had a woman's head. A boy had a short arm and a long one. A woman had a long leg and a short one. An old man had a baby's head; a baby had an old man's.

Horrified at what she had done, Sagabin leaped up and fled. Like a terrified deer, she vanished back into the small compartment in the corner of her father's house. She had ventured out on her own. And something terrible *had* happened.

Mouse Woman—no longer a white mouse— danced up and down in her rage. Raven had won. Raven had indeed won.

In the future, parents would think twice about letting their children be noisy; and the children would think three times about spending half the night wrestling and shouting, or climbing trees and shouting, or playing toss-the-kelp-holdfast and shouting, or even just shouting. And, one of these days, people would start laughing about it in the feasthouses all along the coast and along the rivers, as Raven had planned. It would become yet another famous trick of Raven's.

But that would not be for many, many years. That would not be until long after all the unfortunate people had died. But it would be.

Then, suddenly, her big, busy, mouse eyes narrowed. And her nose twitched. Raven had won. But perhaps she had won, too. For, by doing such an outrageous thing, Raven had shown his arrogant disregard for human beings. So, in the future, no powwow of Supernatural Beings would challenge HER right to handle troublesome young people. By losing, she had won. By winning, Raven had lost. And that was strangely satisfying.

Also, she thought—and now there was a glint of amusement in the big, busy, mouse eyes that looked over the hodgepodge of mixed-up people— there was a certain perverse satisfaction in having people come out right by having them come out all wrong.

Somehow, it made things equal.

4

The Princess and
the Snails

FOR MANY YEARS no princess had vanished.

A number of handsome young people had mysteriously disappeared from totem pole villages, from berry patches, and from fishing stations.

Yet no princess had vanished.

But one was going to.

Mouse Woman knew what was going on. Her big, busy, mouse eyes saw everything. Her busy ears heard everything. And her busy mind could always put two and two together. ("And get five," her neighbors said, shaking their heads over the busiest little busybody in the Place-of-Supernatural-Beings.)

She knew who had captured the handsome young people. She knew who wanted to capture a princess. And she knew who was going to put a stop to those captures.

"Me!" she muttered to herself, without a moment's concern for the size of the Beings she would have to tackle.

"Capture is no way to treat young people," she told herself. "Especially capture that turns them into slaves for those insufferable Super-Snails."

Feeding on pride and on everything else in sight for centuries, the Super-Snails had become as big as whales. Only, unlike whales, they couldn't live in salt water. So their neighbors couldn't drive them off into the sea, where there was more room for such enormous creatures. The Super-Snails stayed where they were, getting more and more monstrous, more and more in need of more and more slaves to cater to their gigantic bodies. And who knew where it would end?

Mouse Woman knew where it ought to end. So, right now, she was going to confront those insufferable Super-Snails in their own house.

There were four of them, with lesser relatives who were only as big as dolphins. There was the chief, Stupendous-Scavenger-and-Supreme-Snail. There was his wife, Magnificent-Mollusca. There was their son, Gigantic-Gastropod. And there was his wife, Gorgeous-Immensity.

Like everyone else in the Place-of-Supernatural-Beings, those four Super-Snails had human shapes in which their spirit selves could move around if they wanted to. But they didn't want to. They had become so proud of their snail magnificence that they never used their human shapes. Except, of course, when Gigantic-Gastropod and Gorgeous-Immensity needed to use theirs to trap unwary young people.

And that was one of the things Mouse Woman intended to see stopped.

She had no trouble getting into their house. As a matter of fact, *they* were the only ones who ever had any trouble getting in and out of that house, the most colossal house in the Place. They had had to have a removable wall built at one end.

She scurried in. And there they were, all as big as whales, with their enormous snail shells rising above their great gray sluggishness: Stupendous-Scavenger-and-Supreme-Snail, Magnificent-Mollusca, Gigantic-Gastropod, and Gorgeous-Immensity. Their monstrous bodies loomed high above her, soft and slithery-slimy.

Mouse Woman glared up at Gorgeous-Immensity. *She* was the one who now wanted a human princess to serve her monstrous appetite.

That was another thing Mouse Woman was going to bring up. Those appetites. The Super-Snails' terrified slaves were stripping the neighborhood to feed them.

Sensing her tiny presence, four pairs of eyes opened to peer through the dimness of the colossal house; four pairs of feelers moved this way and that way.

"I've come to talk to you," Mouse Woman announced in her loudest possible squeak.

"Oh. You." Four pairs of eyes shut. Four pairs of feelers stilled themselves.

"About humans."

Four pairs of eyes opened.

"Humans?" Stupendous - Scavenger - and - Supreme-Snail protested. "Why talk about beings who have never had the good sense to take the Snail as their totem?"

"Or the good taste to use the beauty of a snail to decorate their canoes or their serving bowls or their little goathorn spoons?" Magnificent-Mollusca protested in turn.

"Humans are beneath our notice," Gigantic-Gastropod said.

"Except as slaves," Gorgeous-Immensity added.

"That's what I want to talk about," Mouse Woman squeaked; and her little nose was twitching. "They shouldn't be your slaves."

"Nonsense!" Magnificent-Mollusca answered. "They're very good slaves."

"That's not what I mean. It's bad to snatch young people away from their families."

"Oh, we don't snatch them," Gigantic-Gastropod protested. "They come most willingly."

Mouse Woman's nose twitched again. Of course the young people came most willingly. They thought they were eloping with the handsomest young man or with the most beautiful young woman they had ever seen. For, in their human shapes, the Super-Snails had skin as smooth and lustrous as the pearl lining of a shell.

"It's bad to trap them."

"Bad? Because it's human?" Stupendous-Scavenger-and-Supreme-Snail suggested slyly.

"Human?"

"Certainly. When humans need to eat, *they* trap animals, don't they? With their snares and pits and fishnets. So, when we need to eat, we trap humans. And WE don't even eat THEM," he pointed out, with supreme smugness.

The confrontation was not going exactly as Mouse Woman had planned. And her shoulders sagged under the field mouse blanket.

"Also," Magnificent-Mollusca pointed out, with magnificent smugness, "The happiness of all snails is in our hands. And the snails grow very unhappy when humans kick them off the trail. Or—worse still!—when they don't kick them off the trail, but simply step on their beautiful, fragile, little houses. Horrible humans! It's our duty to punish them."

"You will have noticed," Gigantic-Gastropod pointed out, with gigantic smugness, "we trap only humans who have been cruel to a snail."

"So we are only doing our duty to our beloved snails," Gorgeous-Immensity pointed out. And her smugness was truly immense.

Mouse Woman's nose twitched. Her eyes snapped. And she glared up at Gorgeous-Immensity. "I suppose it's only your duty to your

beloved snails that has you scanning the country-side, waiting for some cruel little princess to step on some poor little snail's house?"

"Of course," Gigantic-Gastropod answered for his wife. "When it's a princess who has vanished, the vanishment gets more publicity. And the *reason* for the vanishment. So there's more chance that more humans will begin to think twice before they kick another snail off a trail, or step on it."

"But won't that do you out of your supply of slaves?" Mouse Woman asked, rather slyly she thought.

"Pfffffffff!" Gigantic-Gastropod's voice was full of unconcern. "We'll never run out of thoughtless, careless humans." He closed his eyes in dismissal of Mouse Woman and her ridiculous ideas.

"We can count on it," Gorgeous-Immensity added, also closing her eyes.

The two biggest Super-Snails didn't bother to say anything before they closed their eyes.

"You haven't heard the last of me," Mouse Woman squeaked at them.

"No. I suppose that would be too much to hope," Magnificent-Mollusca muttered in a sleepy voice.

Mouse Woman marched off to the Trail, where she had made herself Guardian. And *that* was another thing. When those whale-ous creatures or their lesser relatives ventured along the Trail—

blocking passage for everyone else for ages!—they left a glistening path of slime. So they referred to *her* Trail as the Glory-of-Our-Going. Glory, indeed! Mouse Woman's nose twitched. "They haven't seen the last of me," she muttered.

Now, YOU KNOW that the Place-of-Supernatural-Beings was in a thorn-hidden, cliff-ringed valley high in the mountains. You also know that one side of their mountain sloped down to a lake where ducks paddled among the water lilies, where songbirds warbled in the pale aspens along the lake and in the darker pines and spruce trees behind them, and where, at times, the still of the evening was broken by the wild laughter of a loon.

You may not know that another side of that mountain sloped down to the sea. And right at the foot of a particularly steep slope, there was a village. Its carved cedar houses and totem poles stood in an arc, edging the small beach where the canoes were drawn up. And between the brightly decorated houses and the brightly decorated canoes was the main street. The only street, actually.

You also know that all the people belonged to clans: Bear, Raven, Wolf, Frog, Killer-Whale . . .

But you may not know that every family was divided between two clans. For an Eagle could not marry an Eagle. A Wolf could not marry a Wolf. They were too closely related to marry.

So it was that in the biggest house in the village —the house of the Wolf Chief—the princess was an Eagle, like her mother and her five brothers. And, of course, no high-ranking young Eagles were coming to the village to ask if they might marry her.

It seemed, however, that they were the only high-ranking young men along the coast and the river who were *not* coming to the village to ask if they might marry her. For the princess, Alai-l, was as beautiful as a wild rose.

But the Wolf Chief and his Eagle wife did not fancy any of the suitors. None was good enough for *their* daughter. For they were very proud people. And with good reason.

For one thing, both the Chief and his wife wore proud ancient names and proud ancient regalia.

For another, they had six handsome children: four sons who were great sea hunters, one son who was a gifted artist, and a daughter who was a most beautiful young lady.

Also, they were house proud. Their house was enormous. Though a little smaller than the Super-Snails' house, it could have housed several whales (even if the whales would have had some trouble getting in and out through the round opening in the portal pole, especially as there was no water.) And it was full of fine things like carved house posts and painted screens, decorated chests and coppers, sea otter blankets and costly regalia, elegantly carved bowls and goathorn spoons. "What young man could take our princess to so fine a house?" they asked one another.

The street was so littered with disappointed young men that the princess could seldom go out to take the air with her two friends-and-attendants. And she was becoming annoyed. She was longing for escape from the village. In fact, she was becoming so desperate for escape that she was even eyeing her youngest brother's invention—a wooden eagle with moving parts and thongs to make the parts move.

"Why can't you make that thing fly?" she asked him one day, with some impatience.

He was being trained as an artist, a lordly profession in a world where things were made valuable by the beauty of their decoration. But he was spending most of his time working on the eagle that was going to fly. With him in it, he hoped.

Now he gazed at his wooden eagle. "I can make it," he answered his sister in his gentle voice. "But only the Great Eagle Spirit can make it fly." His eyes shone with excitement. For he was sending many prayers to the Great Eagle Spirit.

"Well, get busy!" his sister said; and she moved on. She was out to take the air while the street was temporarily clear of disappointed suitors.

She had reached the end of the street when she saw the snail. Right in her pathway.

These days, there always seemed to be a snail

just where she was going to put her foot. And it was very annoying.

"I suppose YOU came to marry me, too," she said rudely. And she kicked the snail out of the way.

Her two friends stifled their gasps of dismay. It was a bad thing to offend an animal. For who knew what might happen if the animal spirits avenged the offense?

"I've got to get out of this village," Alai-l told them, heading for the beach trail.

"But—" The princess was not allowed to go out of the village without her family around her.

"Stay if you like!" she scolded. "I'm tired of your hovering anyway." And she glided off along the trail.

The girls looked at one another, dismay and uncertainty troubling their faces.

"I'll follow her," one of them said, "while you go and alert the family." But, fearing to further annoy her already annoyed mistress, she followed the princess at a distance. And so it was that, when the princess stopped for some minutes, her follower could not see that a young man was talking to her. He was hidden by a rock.

HE WAS THE HANDSOMEST young man Alai-l had ever seen. He was tall and straight, and his skin seemed as smooth and lustrous as the pearl lining of a shell. So, when he finally held out his hand to her, she took it with strange, dreamlike pleasure. She did give the merest start of surprise at the smoothness of the hand. Then, as if caught in a spell, she glided away with what she sensed was incredible speed.

She had escaped from the village. By elopement with the handsomest of young men. But . . . what was happening to her? Somehow, she had no will but his will. She had to go where he took her. And *where* was he taking her?

By the time she reached the colossal house in the Place-of-Supernatural-Beings, Alai-l's dreamlike pleasure had turned into nightmare. She was gripped by panic. For this was no proper village, with a proper family waiting to welcome a daughter-in-law. She glanced in alarm at the towering cliffs that walled her in.

Then she glanced at the young man.

He was as smooth and as lustrous as the pearl-lining of a shell. He was also as aloof and uncaring. Now he seemed coldly disdainful of the most desired princess in the land.

"This is where you will serve, Slave-Princess," he said, pushing her rudely in.

"Slave-Princess?" she gasped. Then she heard the big, big, terrible, rumbling, churning, bubbling sound.

After the brightness of outdoors, the dimness of the huge, windowless house was terrifying. It was even more terrifying when she made out the three monstrous shapes lying under enormous snail shells. The big, big, terrible, rumbling, churning, bubbling sound was coming from deep inside them. With a gasp of horror, she turned to the young man.

But he had vanished. Where he had been, there was only another monstrous shape lying under another enormous snail shell. And it seemed to sleep, as the other three were sleeping, with a big, big, terrible, rumbling, churning, bubbling sound coming from deep inside it.

Four Super-Snails! Each as big as a whale. Their monstrous bodies loomed high above her, soft and slithery-slimy.

Shuddering with horror, Alai-l cowered back into a dark corner.

At once she felt a tug at her robe. And there was the tiniest of old women, watching her with big, busy, mouse eyes.

"Mouse Woman!" She only breathed it. For the tiniest of old women was holding up a cautioning finger.

"You have woolen ear ornaments?" Mouse Woman asked, though her eyes were already coveting Alai-l's red woolen tassels.

"Yes, Grandmother." Trembling with haste, the princess took them off and handed them to the tiny old woman.

Mouse Woman almost snatched them from her hand. And her ravelly little fingers began tearing them into a lovely, loose, nesty pile of mountain sheep wool. Then, having received her favorite gift, she properly proceeded to give her favorite giving—advice to a young person who had been tricked into trouble.

"Do you know where you are, Princess?"

Alai-l swallowed as she shook her head.

"You are in the house of the Super-Snails in the Place-of-Supernatural-Beings. They captured you because you were cruel to a snail."

Flooded with fear, and with remorse for what she had done, Alai-l remembered the snail she had kicked out of her way. It had been tiny and help-less and harmless; while these—She couldn't bear to look at the monstrous Beings lying soft and slithery-slimy under their enormous snail shells. But she shuddered.

"Do not eat their crabapples," Mouse Woman said, "or you will turn into what they are."

"What . . . they . . . are!" Alai-l darted a horrified glance at them. "Oh, no, Grandmother!" She would never eat their crabapples. Not ever!

Then she sagged in despair.

"Your brothers will search for you," Mouse Woman comforted her.

"But—"

But Mouse Woman had vanished.

Her brothers would search for her. But would they ever find the hidden opening through the wickedly thorny hedge of devil's club? Would

they ever find the trail down? If only they could
see the mountain as the high-circling eagles could
see it! She had a sudden wild thought about her
youngest brother's wooden eagle. "Oh! Make it
fly!" she breathed, closing her eyes. And her words
were a prayer to the Great Eagle Spirit.

BACK IN ALAI-L'S VILLAGE, the alarm spread swiftly.

The princess had vanished.

People searched the houses and the trails. But
there was no sign of her. So her four eldest brothers leaped into canoes with their paddlers. They
raced off to neighboring villages. And soon all the
young men who had desired her were searching
everywhere. But no one could find a trace of the
vanished princess.

The grieving Wolf Chief sent out messengers
to call in the shamans.

They came to the village. They put on dancing
aprons that clattered with fringes of bird beaks.
They put crowns of grizzly bear claws over their
long straggly gray hair. They picked up their medicine rattles and their white eagle tail feathers. And,
as wooden batons and padded hands drummed on
hollow cedar, they began to circle the fire in wild
leaping dances. The dances grew wilder and faster,
wilder and faster, wilder and faster until, one by
one, the shamans collapsed and lay as though dead.

People hushed themselves. For now the shamans' spirit-selves had left their bodies to make

spirit journeys in search of the princess. But not one of them could find her.

Sad chants began to wail through the village. Then a woman shaman arrived from a distant village. "I will find the princess," she told the grieving Wolf Chief.

She put on her dancing apron that clattered with fringes of bird beaks. She put a crown of grizzly bear claws over her long straggly gray hair. She picked up her medicine rattle and her white eagle tail feather. Then, as the box drums throbbed through the great house, she began to circle the fire in a wild leaping dance. Her dance grew wilder and faster, wilder and faster, wilder and faster until, suddenly, she collapsed and lay as though dead.

The house hushed itself. And the people waited, almost holding their breath.

At long, long last she seemed to stir. And the people began to chant softly, luring her spirit-self back to its body.

"I saw the princess," she announced, sitting up. And her eyes were the wild, glittering eyes of one who has seen things that mortals do not see.

People held themselves hushed to hear her.

"The Super-Snails hold her captive in the Place-of-Supernatural-Beings high in the mountains. They captured her because she was cruel to a snail. And now she serves them as their slave."

"Their SLAVE?" her four eldest brothers cried out in horror. And at once they set off with their attendants.

As the days and then the weeks went by, the brothers did not return. And more and more people turned disapproving looks on the youngest brother. For he had not raced off to search for his sister. Instead, he had stayed in the village, working quietly at his wooden eagle; he left only to go to lonely places to fast and pray.

One by one, the brothers returned to the village with their attendants. Not one had found the Place-of-Supernatural-Beings high in the mountains. All had wandered and searched only to be defeated at last by an enormous, impassible wall of wickedly thorny devil's club.

"Now I will go," the youngest brother announced. "And I will find our sister." His voice held a quiet confidence.

People looked askance at him. For how could a mere boy do what men had failed to do? Taking only two boy attendants. And the moving parts of a wooden eagle!

"I will find our sister," the boy repeated, with the same quiet confidence as before.

And off he went.

As the young Eagle prince and his two friends made their way into the mountains, they were careful with the parts of the wooden eagle. At night, when they camped, they ate sparingly and made burnt offerings to the Great Eagle Spirit—offerings of fat and eagle down, of red ochre and blue paint, and of the lime of burned clamshells.

As though in answer to their unceasing prayers, the boys went straight to the cleverly concealed opening in the wall of wickedly thorny devil's club that ringed the cliffs surrounding the hidden valley. And when they had glided through, they stood on the edge of a cliff. Below them stretched an awesome valley, walled on all sides by towering cliffs. Yet there were houses in the valley.

"The Place-of-Supernatural-Beings," the prince said. And his keen artist eyes searched the houses and poles for Snail carvings.

"There it is. That colossal house," he told his attendants. "That is where my sister is captive."

His friends looked with dismay at the sheer walls of the valley. "How shall we get down to her?" they wailed. And neither dared to add, "And then how shall we get up again?"

"I shall fly down in my wooden eagle," the prince assured them. "I shall fly down with the help of the Great Eagle Spirit. While you race home to alert the village. For the Super-Snails are sure to pursue us. Perhaps the men can sharpen hemlock stakes as weapons." Hadn't the woman shaman said that the Super-Snails were as big as whales? "Go swiftly!" he ordered. "And go now!"

So off they went, leaving the prince alone on the cliff with his prayers and his wooden eagle.

While it was still light, he worked carefully, fitting the moving parts together and testing the thongs that moved them. He was waiting for the cover of darkness and the faint light of starshine.

NIGHT FELL on the Place-of-Supernatural-Beings. Rasping tongues stopped eating. And in the colossal house, the great, soft, slithery-slimy monsters settled into sleep. A big, big, terrible, rumbling, churning, bubbling sound filled the darkness.

Exhausted by her day's labors, the princess cowered back in her corner.

Suddenly, she felt a tug at her robe.

"Mouse Woman!" She scarcely breathed it. Then she glanced in terror at the sleeping forms. But they did not stir. The feelers did not move. There was only the big, big, terrible, rumbling, churning, bubbling sound filling the darkness.

Another tug at her robe made her rise quietly and follow the tiny friend-of-young-people out into the starry night.

"Your youngest brother is coming for you," Mouse Woman squeaked. And she pointed to a spot on the top of a cliff.

Alai-l caught her breath. And as she watched, aghast yet wildly hopeful, a mechanical eagle launched itself from the cliff.

"The wooden eagle!" she gasped. "Oh! Make

it fly!" Her words were a prayer to the Great Eagle Spirit.

Almost holding her breath, she watched the big jerky bird soar straight toward her. She saw it land. And the splintering thud of its landing made her glance back in terror. Had the Super-Snails heard it?

Then she was embracing her youngest brother. Her dear gifted brother!

And then her voice was a hushed wail. "My dear! Will it fly up again?"

It was Mouse Woman who answered. "There's no need. You see the glisten of snail slime? That is the Trail. Their Glory-of-Our-Going." Her nose twitched. "Hide the eagle along the way! And hurry! Hurry!"

They needed no second bidding. They were off like two deer. Their horror of what was behind them sped their feet up the glistening Trail and down the mountain.

Because of the denseness of growth on the seaward side of the mountain, they had to circle around on animal trails; they had to follow creek beds.

By midmorning they were along the creek that flowed out to the sea near their village. But they could hear terrible sounds behind them, as if a fire were raging through the forest.

The Super-Snails were coming.

They raced into the village shrieking, "The

Snails are coming! The Snails are coming!" Then
they fell to the ground in utter exhaustion. And
they lay as though dead.

"Put them into a canoe!" the Wolf Chief ordered.

The women and children had already been taken
off to a nearby island. And now the canoes were
ready for the others, ready to take them away
from the Super-Snails if the sharpened hemlock
stakes failed to rout the terrible Beings.

"Listen!" someone screamed.

There was a terrible sound on the mountain,
the sound of rocks rolling and trees crashing.

Horrified eyes turned to the steep, timbered
slope behind the village.

"A landslide!" The weight of the enormous
bodies had started a landslide.

"Into the canoes!" the Wolf Chief ordered.
Hemlock stakes were mere splinters against an
avalanche of trees and rocks and whalous-bodies-
riding-the-slide-down-to-the-sea.

Canoes shot out into deep water. And horrified
eyes watched the avalanche of trees and rocks and
whalous bodies bury the beautiful carved houses
and crest poles. Then they watched the monsters
sink, helpless, in the sea. For land snails could not
live in salt water. The SEA would destroy the Super-
Snails.

A wild wailing rose up from the canoes and
from the nearby island. The Super-Snails were

gone. But so was the beautiful village. It was a punishment from the spirits.

"If only . . ." Alai-l murmured, remembering a small snail.

"If only . . ." a dozen people murmured, remembering many snails. And they knew that, from now on, everyone would think twice before kicking a snail out of the way or stepping on its beautiful little house.

DARKNESS HAD COME AGAIN to the colossal house in the Place-of-Supernatural-Beings. But now there was no movement of enormous feelers. There was no sound of rasping tongues. There was no big, big, terrible, rumbling, churning, bubbling sound coming from deep inside monstrous bodies.

Now there was only the fire flickering through cavernous spaces. There was only a circle of people around the fire, people whose skin was as smooth and as lustrous as the pearl lining of a shell. For of course, the spirit-selves of the Super-Snails had not died. They had returned to the Place to animate their other—their human—shapes.

Now their voices were sad, lamenting their lost immensity.

Then the voice of Magnificent-Mollusca turned angry. "You would have a princess to serve you," she said accusingly to her daughter-in-law.

"Now, now," Stupendous-Scavenger-and-Supreme-Snail protested in a soothing voice. "It is only because it was a princess that the vanishment caused such havoc. It is only because it was a princess that the tale will spread far and wide; and so more people will think twice before they kick another snail out of the way."

"Or step on one of their beautiful, fragile little houses," Gigantic-Gastropod agreed, with a none-too-happy glance at one of the beautiful, fragile little houses *his* spirit self would now have to occupy.

"I've been thinking," the Chief went on. "Now that we have to start all over again with tiny snail bodies, perhaps . . . perhaps I won't need to be quite so stupendous."

"Or I quite so magnificent," his wife agreed, thinking it over.

"I suppose I could be a little less gigantic," Gigantic-Gastropod said. An ungainly body had its drawbacks.

His wife sighed. "I suppose I could be gorgeous without being such an immensity."

A white mouse darted out of a corner and did a merry little scurrying little dance around the fire.

Then Mouse Woman stood before them.

"You!" they all said. And their voices were something less than neighborly.

"I told you you hadn't seen the last of me," she squeaked at them.

Then she vanished.

It was all so strangely satisfying, she thought,

as she marched along to her Trail. The bigness of the Super-Snails had brought them to smallness. And the thoughtlessness of the people had made them thoughtful.

Somehow, it made everything equal.

5

The Princess and
the Geese

ONCE IT WAS a supernatural princess who vanished.
But she had not been tricked into trouble. She had
vanished because she was unhappy about living
with humans.

This is the way it happened.

It was in the time of very long ago, when things
were different in the vast green wildernesses of the
Northwest. It was at a time when Mouse Woman
was living on the Haida islands.

It was early in the spring. Geese were filling the
northern flyway with their wild calls as they
moved toward their summer feeding grounds in
great flying wedges.

A chief's son was out alone, watching the mighty
travellers of the air with longing eyes. For not
even the biggest and finest of the Haida canoes
could venture as far as the great birds. He was
looking up at the birds with shining eyes when

he heard a chattering of geese at a nearby lake.
Eager to observe the mighty visitors at close
range, he glided warily toward the sound. But there
were no geese. There were only two maidens
swimming near the shore. They were swimming
and laughing and chattering merrily.

The young man caught his breath. For there
was something geeselike about the chattering.
And, shining silver in the sun, two large gooseskins lay at the edge of the lake.

"Goose maidens!" He scarcely breathed it. For
these were supernatural maidens. Narnauks. And
they were as beautiful as a summer sky.

He longed to speak to them. But he knew that
they would take flight at the first sign of a human
being. Unless— His eyes widened with a thought.
The goose maidens could not take flight without
their flying blankets. He crept warily toward the
gooseskins.

A startled cry told him he was discovered.

Wild to speak to the two beautiful maidens, he
threw himself down on the gooseskins so that they
could not take them.

The elder maiden came at him, hissing like an
outraged gander. But the younger maiden only
looked shyly at him.

Caught in the spell of her eyes, the youth rose
to his feet, picking up the gooseskins.

The elder maiden almost snatched hers from
his hand. But the younger one stood looking
at him with great wondering eyes. And a wild

thought leaped up in the young man. Perhaps she would marry him.

With the courage born of his yearning, he held her gooseskin out toward her. "If you will marry me, Princess, I will give you your flying blanket."

The elder maiden hissed in outrage at such presumption. "Marry you? You! A mere human!" But the younger one still looked at him.

"I will marry you," she whispered.

The elder maiden hissed at both of them. Angrily she put on her gooseskin. And then she was a goose, flapping furiously out into the lake. With a great thunder of wings and a fury of wild calls, she rose. She flew up, up, up, up until she was lost in the vast blueness of the sky.

"She has gone home to Skyland," the younger maiden whispered. And her shining eyes were shadowed with concern.

"I will take you home to my village," he assured her. "You will be warmly welcomed by my family." But now a shadow darkened *his* eyes. For the beautiful princess was a narnauk. His family would look askance at her. Unless they did not know she was a narnauk.

Putting her flying blanket on the ground, the youth took off his top martenskin robe and laid it gently on her shoulders. Then he folded up her gooseskin and hid it under his second robe. "May we keep this as our secret, Princess?" he begged.

The goosemaiden nodded, though her eyes were still anxious.

They started toward the village. And when they were nearing it, the youth hid the supernatural gooseskin in the heart of an old cedar tree.

"Keep it safe!" the maiden murmured to the tree. The youth looked at her with a moment's sadness. "You will be so happy with my family that you will not want it again, Princess."

For a time she was happy with his human family. Her husband could see the questions in his parents' eyes. But they were a proud and proper people. They did not pry into their daughter-in-law's concerns. They recognized the nobility in her bearing and in her manners. They noted the richness of her broad black neck ring. Obviously she was a princess who had been spirited away from her own people and was now keeping herself secret from some dreaded enemy. But she did walk a little oddly, they confessed to one another.

"Since my wife came in springtime, with the geese," her husband suggested, "let us call her Goose Princess." He caught her grateful and loving glance.

Food was her first problem; for she did not like their food, until a woman chanced to steam the roots of plants she had gathered near the mouth of the creek. Goose Princess ate those with relish. "Though I do wish they weren't cooked," she confided to her husband.

For some time, she seemed happy enough in her new home.

Then her husband began to notice something. Often at night she glided silently out of the house. And when she returned she was cold. Cold as the night air. Cold as the seawater. One night he stealthily followed her. He saw her take her supernatural flying blanket from the heart of the cedar tree. He watched her fly off to graze on sea grasses. And as he went back to the house so that she would not know he had watched her, his heart was heavy. Goose Princess was not satisfied to be a human.

Summer passed. And winter came. A desperately cold winter. Fierce gales uprooted trees and set the sea smoking with blown spray. Canoes could not go out on the sea for food. Snow and ice locked in the land. And people in the great cedar houses grew hungry. For, in the Haida islands, no one was prepared for such a winter.

One day when they were outdoors, Goose Princess said, "Sʜ!" to her husband. And she seemed to listen to the sky; though he could hear nothing but the wind. "My father is sending food to us," she told him.

To the amazement of the whole village, a great flying wedge of geese came out of the south. And when they had gone, there was a mound of roots and grasses behind the house where Goose Princess lived.

"Strange food for *people!*" envious neighbors muttered. There was fear and scorn—as well as envy—in their voices. For people do not like unaccountable happenings.

Again and again during the bitter winter, flying wedges of geese came out of the south, bringing more roots and grasses for the princess's family. "That family will be turning into gaggling geese," a man muttered. And his friends laughed. For there was now much gossip in the village. There were sly little goose walks and goose hisses. And there were many sidelong glances at the mysterious princess who had come from no-one-knew-where. She did walk very oddly, people whispered to one another.

Goose Princess heard the whispers. She caught the sidelong glances and the sly little goose walks and goose hisses. "They are mocking me," she told her husband. And for the very first time, she hissed at him. "They are mocking me; for humans are always suspicious of people who are different." Then her eyes blazed with anger. "And they are mocking the geese, who are greater than they are." She raced out of the house. But, after a while, she came back.

Then the worst of the storms was over. It was early in the spring. Geese filled the northern flyway with their wild calls as they moved toward their summer feeding grounds in great flying wedges. And as she watched their high passing, Goose Princess was sad and quiet. Her eyes were full of yearning.

One night, she slipped out of the house.

Alarmed by what might happen, her husband

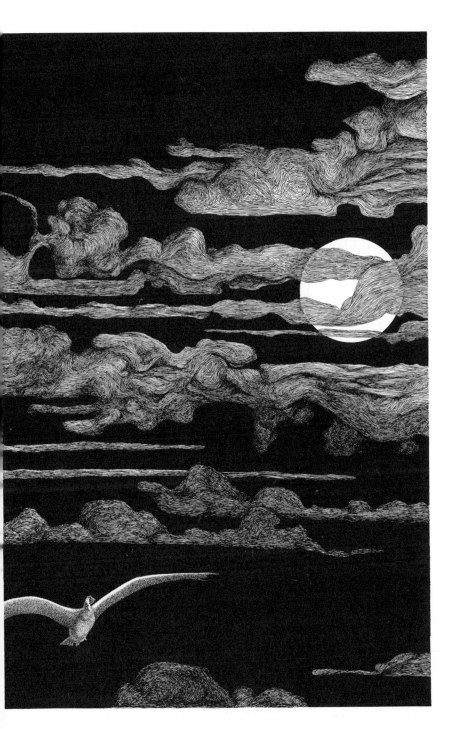

followed her. But she seemed to fly on the wings of her longing for her own kind. And as he fell farther behind, she reached the cedar tree. With a quick, grateful word to the tree, she snatched up her supernatural gooseskin and put it on. Then, with a great thunder of wings and a trumpeting of wild calls, she rose. She flew up, up, up, up until she was lost in the vast darkness of the sky.

Her husband sank to the ground in despair. He knew he had lost his beautiful goose princess.

At long last, he went sadly back to the village.

Next day, the rumors flashed from house to house. Goose Princess had vanished as mysteriously as she had come.

"She was not a proper woman," people whispered to one another. And now there was fear in their voices. For they had offended a narnauk. And who knew what would happen to them? They began to turn angry glances on the young man who had brought the narnauk to their village. It was his fault that they were now in danger.

The young man neither heard the whispers nor saw the glances. For he was lost in grief.

When he finally stirred himself, he made his way to the remote house of a shaman, a witch doctor who had almost left the ways of man to have closer contact with the spirit world.

"My wife has vanished," the young man told the shaman. "So I wish to find the Trail to her father's village."

The old man's glittering eyes seemed to pierce into the young man's innermost being. "Your wife's father is a Great One almost beyond the thinking of a human being," he said in his strange, old, cracked voice.

The young man nodded. He knew that his father-in-law was a Supernatural Being. "Where is the Trail to his village?" he insisted.

The old medicine man pierced him again with his glittering wild eyes before he said, "You are a worthy man. The Trail runs behind my house."

Pausing only long enough to present the old shaman with a small, but beautifully carved box, the young man raced out to seek the Trail, the Spirit Trail that would lead him to Skyland.

Growth was so dense on the Haida islands that men seldom ventured into the depth of the forest; they clung to the seacoast. But now a Trail seemed to open before him as he moved. And it closed behind him.

His heart was pounding. For who knew what would happen along such a Trail? He pushed from his mind the old stories of fearsome Beings who lived there.

As he moved along the Trail, he seemed to have left even time behind him. For his world was a world of summer.

He had gone a long, long way when he came upon the mouse. A white mouse! It had cranberries in its mouth. And it was vainly trying to get over a huge tree that had fallen across its pathway.

With instant compassion for the small creature, he picked it up and lifted it over the fallen tree. He watched it scurry off into a stand of large ferns.

Then he heard a voice, a squeaky little voice. "Come in and speak to the Chief-woman!" it commanded.

Startled by the words, the young man lifted a leaning fern. And there, to his amazement, was a house. A huge, underground house.

"Come in!" It was a sharp command in the same squeaky voice.

He went in. And there was the tiniest of old women cooking cranberries in a hot-stone box. She was watching him with big, busy, mouse eyes.

"You are a worthy man," she said to him in the same sharp voice. "And since you have helped me, I will help you. Though it is not a proper marriage," she added tartly.

"It is a marriage, Grandmother," he protested.

"It is a marriage," she conceded. "And I owe you assistance." For of course, this was Mouse Woman. And of course Mouse Woman knew the obligation of a gift. If help had been given, the helper must be compensated.

She marched off to a corner of her house and began to open a nest of five carved chests. From the innermost chest, she took out a tiny mouse-skin.

"I wore this for hunting when I was young," she told him, with just a little sigh for her long gone days of hunting. She held it out to him.

"Wear it!" she commanded.

"Wear . . . that?" The young man looked at the tiny mouseskin. He looked at his own big body.

"Wear it!" she repeated.

To humor her, he took the mouseskin. And to his utter amazement, he could enter it the way the reflection of a giant tree can enter a tiny puddle. He could move around in it, as if he were a mouse.

"Practice wearing it!" she commanded. And she pointed toward the outdoors.

The young man, now seeming to be a mouse, scampered around logs and mosses for a brief time. Then he went back into the house.

"Now," the tiny old woman said, "as soon as you have eaten, be on your way! Though it is not a proper marriage."

"It is a marriage, Grandmother," he answered.

Removing the supernatural garment, the young man ate and went on his way.

This time he met only one creature—a strange little man with one leg, one arm, and half a head.

"Master Hopper!" he gasped, watching the half-man hop boisterously around the base of a red pole that seemed to reach up and up forever, beyond the highest treetops. He had heard about Master Hopper, but he had not believed in him.

Then his gaze fastened on the pole. He had heard stories about that, too, and had scarcely believed them. *This* was the red pole that reached up to Skyland. Where Goose Princess was.

Without a moment's hesitation, he entered his magical mouseskin and scampered up the red pole. He climbed up and up and up beyond the treetops, up and up and up beyond the eagles, up and up and up beyond the clouds, up and up and up until he reached the door into Skyland.

It was an alarming door. It opened, and shut again, as fast as the blink of an eye. He watched it for a long time. And only when he had caught the rhythm of its opening, did he ready himself to leap through.

As a mouse, he leaped through.

Then, as a man, he looked about him.

Skyland was dazzling. Houses as blue as the sky and as white as the clouds were decorated with tiny stars.

Before the biggest house, he saw the Goose pole.

Then he saw Goose Princess running toward him. Goose Princess was embracing him. She was taking him into the house of her father who was Town Chief.

"You will be happy here," she told him.

And for some time, he was happy.

Then he began to long for the great sea where he had gone sea-hunting. He began to long for the smell of the cedars, the scream of the seagulls, the sound of the rain on the roof. He began to long for his family.

"My son-in-law is not happy here," the Town Chief told his daughter.

She nodded in sad agreement. "He is not happy here." As she had not been happy living among humans.

"I will send him back to his own kind," the Town Chief told her. And again she nodded in sad agreement. She understood his yearning for his own kind.

The Town Chief summoned Eagle and Raven and Heron and Seagull to consult about the manner of the young man's return to earth. And it was agreed that they could carry him back while he was sleeping.

So IT WAS THAT the young man woke up next morning in his own house in his own village.

"Did I dream it all?" he asked himself, glancing about at the familiar walls and smokehole.

Then he saw the mouseskin. And he reached out a hand for it.

But as he reached, the mouseskin vanished.

He blinked his eyes to clear them.

But the mouseskin had truly vanished. And he thought he heard a small, sharp-voiced mutter, "It was not a proper marriage."

INDEED, IT WAS NOT a proper marriage. But, as long as he lived, the Goose Princess's husband watched the high passing of the geese with a great yearning. He went often to lonely waters. But he never again found a goose maiden swimming.

6

The Princess and the Magical Hat

It was in the days of very long ago, when things were different.

Then, supernatural beings roamed the vast green wildernesses of the Northwest Coast. And one of those most feared by the seagoing people was Great-Whirlpool-Maker, who lived on a remote island and haunted the waters. His terrifying power was in his hat.

Now this magical hat was woven of spruce roots, like ordinary hats. It had an ordinary design of killer whales. But instead of being topped by several plain woven rings, like the hats of great chiefs, it was woven into a towering spiral. And instead of being rounded off at the top like ordinary hats, it was woven into a deep well and topped by a living surf bird. When the bird spun itself about, it started a whirling of the magical water in the well. And then, when the bird flew off, it released a terrible, whirling power that could suck down even the greatest of the great northern canoes as if it were nothing but a bit of driftwood.

The seagoing people of the north moved in awe of Great-Whirlpool-Maker. They were careful never to spit into the sea or to do anything else that might offend the spirits of the ocean. For who knew when Great-Whirlpool-Maker might wreak vengeance on them?

Now, as well as his terrifying hat, Great-Whirlpool-Maker had bad eyes, a keen nose, a taste for human beings, and a very stupid son.

Son-of-Great-Whirlpool-Maker was so muddleheaded that he wanted to marry a human princess, when obviously such a marriage would keep his father licking his lips in agony every time he glanced at his daughter-in-law. For, of course, not even Great-Whirlpool-Maker could eat his own daughter-in-law.

"Stupid son," his father said almost daily, "you must not marry a human princess."

"Why not?" his son answered almost daily, proving his muddleheadedness, if such proof had been needed. And he kept his big ears alert for word of a suitably beautiful princess.

Now YOU KNOW THAT, in the days of very long ago, totem pole villages edged many of the lonely beaches of the Northwest Coast. Standing with their backs to big, snow-capped mountains, the villages were bright with the carved and painted emblems of the clans. Their crested canoes dared the wild western rivers; they threaded the wild maze of off-shore islands; they ranged the wild coast.

In one such village, in the biggest of the big cedar houses, lived a princess called Slender-One. And in the way of the northern people, this princess was expected to marry her father's nephew and heir. (For, of course, her father and *his* relatives belong to a different clan from her mother and her brothers, for marriage arrangements.) But so beautiful was Slender-One that high ranking young men from many villages came to her village with much ceremony to ask if she would marry them.

One day such a suitor arrived with ten canoes full of relatives. And the relatives came in their most magnificent regalia, dancing on cedar planks that had been laid across the canoes. Yet Slender-One's mother and two brothers and three uncles shook their heads and said, "No."

Later, another such suitor arrived with ten canoes full of relatives. Again the relatives came in their most magnificent regalia, dancing on cedar planks that had been laid across the canoes. And again Slender-One's mother and two brothers and three uncles shook their heads and said, "No."

Later, yet another such suitor arrived with ten

canoes full of relatives. Again the relatives came in their most magnificent regalia, dancing on cedar planks that had been laid across the canoes. And yet again Slender-One's mother and two brothers and three uncles shook their heads and said, "No."

Then another suitor arrived. But this one came alone in a sealskin canoe. And this time Slender-One's mother and two brothers and three uncles and everyone else in the village gasped in terror. For a sealskin canoe meant a supernatural suitor. And this one was wearing a towering hat with a living surf bird on top.

"It's Son-of-Great-Whirlpool-Maker," people muttered. And they trembled with terror. They didn't want the princess to marry into that family. But how could a seagoing people dare to offend a family with a hat that could release a power that could suck down even the greatest of the great northern canoes as if it were no more than a bit of driftwood?

There was one wild hope.

Son-of-Great-Whirlpool-Maker was stupid.

"Perhaps we can substitute a slave girl for Slender-One," her mother dared to hope. "He'd never know the difference."

Slender-One had ten slave girls. Her relatives dressed one of them in fine clothes. And, with much ceremony, they escorted her down to the beach.

Son-of-Great-Whirlpool-Maker was indeed

stupid. In fact, on this occasion, he had been muddleheaded enough to take a hat he couldn't handle
—his father's magical hat. It rose above his big
ears in a towering swirl. On top of it sat the living
surf bird, who was very annoyed with the whole
proceeding. The bird was so annoyed that it kept
flying off the hat in a way that terrified its wearer
even more than it terrified the people of the village.
For, of course, Son-of-Great-Whirlpool-Maker
had certainly not intended to do anything with the
hat, except impress people.

Son-of-Great-Whirlpool-Maker was indeed
stupid. But the surf bird was not. So when the
slave girl arrived on the beach in fine clothes, pretending to be the princess, the surf-bird squawked,
"K-NO!"

Son-of-Great-Whirlpool-Maker was far too terrified of the bird to go against its wishes. So he
too squawked, "K-NO!"; though he couldn't see
why he was refusing to marry such a beautiful
princess.

Slender-One had ten slave girls. So ten times
her relatives dressed one of them in fine clothes
and escorted her, with much ceremony, down to
the beach. Ten times the surf bird squawked,
"K-NO!" And ten times Son-of-Great-Whirlpool-
Maker also squawked, "K-NO!"; though he still
couldn't see why he was refusing to marry such a
beautiful princess.

"What can we do?" Slender-One's relatives
wailed to one another. They did not want the

princess to marry into that family. But how could a seagoing people dare to offend a family with a hat that could release a power that could suck down even the greatest of the great northern canoes as if it were no more than a bit of driftwood? " What can we do?" they wailed.

It was what they had already done that enraged the surfbird. Suddenly, it started spinning around. The magical water beneath it began to whirl. And when the bird flew off, suddenly, the released power started a mighty whirlpool offshore. On shore, it started a whirling of pebbles and driftwood and even canoes.

The people were terrified.

So was Son - of - Great - Whirlpool - Maker. For pebbles and driftwood and even canoes were hurtling around his muddled head. "Do something! Do something!" he yelled at the surf bird, who was calmly watching proceedings from the top of a totem pole.

Naturally, the people thought he was yelling at them. So they did something. They fled into the house, grabbed the princess and brought her out, with her ten slave girls.

At once the whirling stopped. And the surf bird settled itself once more on the magical hat.

With more haste than ceremony, her relatives escorted the princess down to the beach and fled back into the house. So they did not even see which way the canoe went.

And they did not see how the next great whirling

started, or where. They only heard a few thumps against the planks of the big cedar house. And when they finally dared to venture out into the quiet that followed the thumps, they found only a bit more damage than there had been before.

There was no sign of the sealskin canoe. No sign of the princess. No sign of the ten slave girls. The princess had vanished.

A wild wailing rose up from the beach, where Slender-One's relatives began mourning the loss of their beautiful princess.

Then someone saw the hat, the magical hat.

It was on top of a totem pole.

The wailing was lost in the stunned quiet of dismay.

Blown from a muddled head by the whirlwind it had created somewhere offshore, the terrifying hat had landed on the totem pole. And there it sat, with the living surf bird at the top.

Like a beached whale, the hat was now theirs. Sent to them by the spirits, in return for the princess they had given to a spirit being?

People looked at one another in dismay. By the custom of the Coast, the hat was now theirs. But who wanted a hat topped by a bird no one knew how to handle? Who wanted a hat that had already wrecked their beach?

There was one wild hope.

Great-Whirlpool-Maker would undoubtedly want it back.

"Perhaps we can give him back the hat,"
Slender-One's mother dared to hope. "And he will
give us back the princess." After all, the obligation of a gift was a law of the Northwest. If the
villagers gave Great-Whirlpool-Maker the magical hat, he had to give them something of even
greater value. His pride demanded it, and his prestige among his peers. And in this case, it would
mean getting rid of something they certainly did
not want—the hat—in return for something they
certainly did want—the princess.

But, who would dare to touch the hat? And risk
annoying the surf bird? Even if someone did dare
to touch it, who would dare to take it to Great-
Whirlpool-Maker, who had a taste for human beings? And even if someone did dare to take it to
him, who knew where he lived?

People eyed the surf bird, who was calmly
watching proceedings from the top of the totem
pole. And their eyes were uneasy. Something had
to be done.

But what?

Clearly, there was only one way to find out.

A shaman put on a dancing apron that clattered
with fringes of bird beaks. He put a crown of
grizzly bear claws over his long straggly gray
hair. He picked up his medicine rattle and his white
eagle tail feather. Then, as wooden batons and
padded hands drummed on hollow cedar, he began to circle the fire in a wild leaping dance. The

dance grew faster and wilder, faster and wilder, faster and wilder until, suddenly, the shaman collapsed and lay as though dead.

People hushed themselves. For now the shaman's spirit-self had left its body to make the spirit journey in search of Great-Whirlpool-Maker's house. And who knew what it would find on such a journey? Almost holding their breath, the people waited.

At long, long last the shaman seemed to stir. So the people began to chant softly, luring his spirit-self back to its body.

The shaman sat up. And his eyes were a wild glitter.

"The house is on an island to the north," he said in his cracked old voice. "An island with three bony trees high on a rock. Great-Whirlpool-Maker is wild with anger at the loss of his magical hat; for his power is in that hat. His son does not know where it went. And the princess is lying as though dead in a cave near the house." He held up a scrawny hand to silence the gasps. "Slender-One's mother must go there. Only she must go. And without the hat."

"Without the hat?" People widened their eyes in dismay. The terrible hat was going to stay on in their village? As one, they turned toward the princess's mother.

Slender-One's mother shrank back for one instant. Then, being a great lady, she squared her shoulders to do what must be done. She rose quietly and summoned a slave paddler.

"Take this!" the shaman said; and he gave her an ancient charm shaped like a killer whale. "Tie it to a spear. And cast the spear at a giant killer whale that will surface near your canoe."

The lady tied the charm to a spear. She went off in a small canoe with her slave paddler. And no sooner had they rounded the point to the north than a giant killer whale surfaced near their canoe. The woman cast the spear at it. It seemed to catch the spear in its great mouth. Then it raced northward with the canoe in tow. It went like a storm wind. And, it seemed, before they had really caught their breath again, they were nearing a remote island with three bony trees high on a rock.

The supernatural killer whale made straight for a small lonely beach on the island. It spat out the spear, and vanished.

And there on the beach, appearing as if from nowhere, stood a tiny old woman.

"Mouse Woman!" Slender-One's mother gasped in great relief. For it was well known that Mouse Woman was a friend to the distressed. She always turned up when a princess had vanished.

"You have woolen ear ornaments?" the tiny being asked; though her eyes were already coveting the mother-of-pearl trimmed tassels.

Trembling with haste, the lady took them off and handed them to the little old woman, whose ravelly fingers began at once to tear them into a lovely, loose, nesty pile of mountain sheep wool. Then, having received her favorite gift, Mouse Woman properly proceeded to give her favorite giving—advice.

"Follow me with great stealth," she advised. And she led the way to the cave where Slender-One lay as though dead, without her slave girls. "Leave her there until the hat is returned," Mouse Woman advised.

Then she led the way, by a back entrance, into a great cedar house. She cautioned silence to the two human beings as they cowered back into a dark corner. For, as everyone knew, the huge man by the fire had a taste for human beings. And a keen nose to smell them out.

"I smell human beings!" he cried out. And the two trembled with terror, as Mouse Woman had intended that they should. For it was always a good thing to make a dangerous situation clear to people. Then they were willing to act in the proper manner. And let *her* handle things.

"I SMELL HUMAN BEINGS!"

"Of course you smell human beings," Mouse Woman answered, marching boldly up to the huge man. "The least breath of air stirs the robes of the ten slave girls you ate." She pointed to the ten shredded-cedar-bark robes hanging on the wall. "The smell of the girls lingers."

Great-Whirlpool-Maker considered that explanation. It seemed to almost satisfy him. But he did keep glancing about. And he did keep sniffing in a way that was most disconcerting to the two human beings cowering back in the dark corner.

"I have word of the hat," Mouse Woman announced in her squeaky little voice.

"The hat?" Great-Whirlpool-Maker roared in a voice that made the two human beings jump. He leaped to his feet. "Bring my hat to me!"

"It is not mine to bring," Mouse Woman calmly informed him. "Neither is it yours to demand. For the spirits have given it to a human family."

"What family?" he demanded; and his voice was like a clap of thunder. For his power was in that hat. Without it he was nothing in the world of supernatural beings.

"It is enough for me to know what family," Mouse Woman calmly told him. "Since I will conduct the negotiations."

"Negotiations?" Now his voice was like a long roll of thunder.

"Certainly. Negotiations," said the tiniest but most proper of the narnauks. "Now, if the family were willing to give you the magical hat, what could you give them in return?"

Hope sprang up in his eyes. "My son?" he suggested.

Mouse Woman dismissed that suggestion with a twitch of her nose. So his glance began to range over the treasures in his house.

But Mouse Woman stopped that. Quickly. Before he should peer into a certain dark corner. "You have a princess," she suggested. It was well known that she had a feeling for princesses. "The princess!" His eyes brightened. His tongue licked his big lips.

"A princess alive and in good condition," the tiny negotiator said, to take his mind off his taste for human beings. "Perhaps the family would be willing to accept a princess—IF she were alive and in good condition."

"They can have her," he agreed. In fact, he would be glad to be rid of the human being his son was determined to marry. For the princess's tender flesh was a terrible temptation. It was such a temptation that he had thought grease into the girl's mind to keep her as though dead, well away from his nose. For even he could not eat his own daughter-in-law.

"Do nothing until I return!" Mouse Woman ordered. He had thought grease into the girl's mind; and only he could think it out again. But she did not want him going near the princess until she was there to handle things. "Do nothing until I return!" she ordered again. Then she vanished.

Back once more in the corner with the two human beings, she took a cautious glance at Great-Whirlpool-Maker. But he was rubbing his hands in excitement. He was lost in thoughts of the magical hat. So she whisked the two out the back entrance and led them to their canoe. She got on board with them. "Only I can handle this situation," she told them with proper pride. And when the slave paddler had taken them out into deep water, she took a strange little fish charm out of her handbasket. She tied it to the bow of the canoe and then threw it into the sea, ahead of them.

At once the canoe raced southward. As if it were being towed by a supernatural sea serpent. They stopped once on the way to the village, at a rocky point where four mice were waiting.

"Fetch Great-Charmer to Slender-One's village!" Mouse Woman called out. And the four mice vanished as if they were four wisps of sea mist. "Great-Charmer is one of my best friends," Mouse Woman explained. "And she has agreed to help us." She did not explain *how* Great-Charmer was going to help them.

The canoe sped southward to the village. And there, Slender-One's mother told the people what had happened.

All eyes turned admiringly on valiant little Mouse Woman.

"We will go for the princess tomorrow," the tiny narnauk announced. She indicated Slender-One's mother and two brothers and three uncles. All six swallowed when they thought of what was waiting with the princess.

"And we will take the hat," Mouse Woman went on.

Now everyone swallowed. For who would dare to touch the hat to get it off the totem pole? And who would dare to carry it across the sea, when, at any moment, its living surf bird might spin about, fly off, and release the power that could suck down even the greatest of the great northern canoes as if it were no more than a bit of driftwood?

They all went into the house, where they ate little and talked even less.

Suddenly, the room seemed to brighten. Yet no one had stirred up the fire or thrown on grease to make it flame up.

"Great-Charmer!" Mouse Woman announced in her loudest, proudest squeak. For her best friend was a tall, dazzling lady. And she was wearing the HAT.

People caught their breath. And few slept well that night. For what if the surf bird spun round while they were sleeping, sending firebrands and maybe even people whirling about the great house? What if even the house itself were whirled out to sea, with them in it? When they finally did sleep, they dreamed of carved chests and hot-stone baskets and painted screens flying about their heads.

They were thankful for morning. And never had every last person in the village been so helpful about getting a group out to sea. Never had they watched a departing canoe with more anxious eyes. And never had they seen a being as dazzling as Great-Charmer, sitting serenely in the great, high-prowed canoe with the terrifying hat on her head.

Never had they watched a bird with such concern for its movements.

As before, Mouse Woman tied her fish charm to the bow. As before, she cast it into the water, ahead of the canoe. And exactly as before, the canoe sliced through the water as if it were being towed by a supernatural sea serpent.

Almost, it seemed, before they had caught their breath, the travellers stood off the remote island with three bony trees high on a rock. But this time they stood off the spot where Great-Whirlpool-Maker waited.

He peered at them with his bad eyes. And he almost danced with frustration at being so near the magical hat, and yet so far from it. He watched Great-Charmer step up onto the plank with the hat swirling up above her head to the top, where the living surf bird was enjoying the proceedings.

The first voice to break the tense silence was a small squeaky voice. "Send out a small canoe!"

Great-Whirlpool-Maker raised his hand in a signal. A sealskin canoe moved itself out to the great painted canoe.

Slender-One's two brothers got into it. And, as if silently commanded, the sealskin canoe took them to the beach, where they immediately made for the cave where their sister was lying as though dead.

Great-Whirlpool-Maker's eyes were still peering out at the dazzling lady with the hat. He still

almost danced with frustration. For without that
hat he was nothing among the supernatural beings.
It was Mouse Woman's imperious squeak that
made him finally glance over to where the brothers
were now carrying their limp sister. He licked his
lips at sight of three delicious young people.

"No princess, no hat!" Mouse Woman thun-
dered as well as a small squeaky voice could
thunder. And her nose twitched.

He glared at the little busybody. But he understood her. If he were given the hat he wanted so
much, then he must give, in return, something
the giver wanted quite as much. His pride demanded it.

"A princess in good condition!" Mouse Woman
reminded him.

He glared again at her. But he understood her. If
he were given something of great value, prestige
demanded that he return something of great value.
And, in her present condition, the princess was of
little value.

He glared one last time at the little busybody,
who could be counted on to spread the word of his
behavior. Then, covering his eyes with both hands,
he thought the grease out of Slender-One's mind.

There was a gasp of pleasure from the big canoe
as the princess stirred and then embraced her
brothers.

There was no gasp from Great-Whirlpool-
Maker or his stupid son. One was too busy licking
his lips to gasp; while the other was too busy blink-

ing his eyes as he tried to understand what was happening around him.

Then Son-of-Great-Whirlpool-Maker, like his father, fixed his gaze on the dazzling lady. For he saw that Great-Charmer was much more beautiful than a human princess. He even saw that his father would not always be licking his lips over such a daughter-in-law; for she was not a human being. He didn't even bother to watch the brothers lift his intended bride into the sealskin canoe and then hand her tenderly over to her mother and to her three uncles.

Great-Charmer still stood on the plank, with the magical hat on her head. Great-Whirlpool-Maker still kept his gaze on the hat. And now beads of moisture stood out on his huge forehead. For that hat held his power. And a tiny, meddling busybody was keeping it from him.

He glared at Mouse Woman. *He* had given a gift of great value, hadn't he? Now didn't the receivers' pride demand that they give him something of great value? Wasn't the obligation of a gift the law of the Northwest? A matter of pride! A matter of prestige!

He almost held his breath as Mouse Woman readied her fish charm.

Slender-One and her family, also, almost held theirs. Would Mouse Woman risk giving that inhuman monster his power while they were still near him?

Still almost holding their breath, they watched

her nod to Great-Charmer, who stepped lightly into the sealskin canoe, still wearing the magical hat. And they would have seen what happened next if Mouse Woman hadn't chosen that very moment to toss her fish charm into the sea and set them racing homeward.

They let out their breath in a great sigh of relief. Of course! They should have known that Mouse Woman would honor the obligation of a gift, on their behalf. Of course she would do the proper thing. It was why she was such a power in the world. It was why even the biggest of the narnauks eyed her with respect.

THAT NIGHT, grease flamed up the fire in the great cedar house in Slender-One's village. Delicious whiffs of food tickled people's noses. And fringes of bird beaks and deer hooves clattered as dancing blankets and dancing aprons whirled around the fire.

Then, on a signal from the High Chief, the house hushed itself. And with great ceremony, Slender-One's two brothers approached Mouse Woman with a small dancing apron, beautifully patterned in the Chilkat way. They dropped it around her shoulders, where it became a dancing blanket—a dancing blanket that whirled and clattered as she did a merry, scurrying dance around the leaping fire.

Then she vanished.

No one saw her reappear near a small tidal pool on the beach. No one saw her stoop down to look closely into the small circle of water. No one heard her delighted sigh at seeing the pool hold the whole great starry world in its smallness.

Then, alone with the starry night and the shining water and the deep, deep shadows of the crowding forest, Mouse Woman did another little dance. For it was all strangely satisfying. Through her alert care for young people, the princess was safe. And through equally alert care for proper behavior, the whole village was properly in awe of the mighty world of spirits. With Great-Whirlpool-Maker once more in possession of his magical hat, even the brashest of young paddlers would not dare to spit into the sea or to do anything else that might offend the ocean spirits. As the tiny pool held the whole great starry world in its smallness, so SHE held the balance of the vast green wilderness in her ravelly fingers.

Suddenly they began to almost nibble at the beautifully woven wool of her dancing blanket.

And that, too, was strangely satisfying.

MOUSE WOMAN

Mouse Woman must have been dear to the hearts of the old storytellers in the feasthouses of the Northwest. For, though she seems to have no story of her own, she darted in and out of the tales of many other characters.

I first found her in *Tsimshian Mythology* by Franz Boas, based on texts recorded by Henry Teit, in the *Thirty-First Annual Report of the Bureau of American Ethnology to the Secretary of the Smithsonian Institution 1909–1910*.

Then, searching out this elusive little narnauk, I came upon her again in *Haida Texts and Myths* recorded by John R. Swanton for the Smithsonian Institution Bureau of American Ethnology, Bulletin 29, Washington: Government Printing Office, 1905.

The stories in this book are based on material in those two scholarly volumes.